The program is well conceived, composed of reader-friendly explanations of English expressions and grammar, quizzes to help the student learn vocabulary and understand the meaning of the texts, and fabulous illustrations that adorn every page. In addition, with our "Guide to Listening," not only is reading comprehension enhanced but also listening comprehension skills are highlighted.

In the audio recording of the book, texts are vividly read by professional American voice actors. The texts are rewritten, according to the levels of the readers by an expert editorial staff of native speakers, on the basis of standard American English with the ministry of education recommended vocabulary. Therefore, it will be of great help even for all the students that want to learn English.

Please indulge yourself in the fun of reading and listening to English through *Let's Enjoy Masterpieces*.

杜蘭朵公主 Opera *Turandot*

Turandot is an opera of Puccini, an Italian composer (1858–1924) famous for *Tosca* and *Madam Butterfly*. *Turandot* was the last and most grand opera of Puccini.

Set in China in legendary times in Peking, the opera tells the story of the cold-hearted princess Turandot, who executed all her suitors for failing to answer three riddles that she posed and about how the prince of the kingdom of Tartary melted Turandot's icy heart and helped her realize the meaning of true love.

In 1920, Puccini decided to make the fairytale Turandotte, written by the Italian author Carlo Gozzi in the 18th century, into an opera. Puccini was enchanted by the story's background because it took place during legendary times of exotic and mythic China. However, Puccini died before completing the three-act opera. Afterwards, Franco Alfano, Puccini's friend and colleague, completed the final scene.

On April 25th, 1926, the historic premiere of *Turdandotte* was given at Teatro alla Scala, conducted by Toscanini. In the performance of the premiere, after conducting Act III, up to the death of Liu, written by Puccini, Toscanini laid down his baton and faced the audience with the words, "Here ends the opera left unfinished by the Maestro, because at this point the Maestro died". It remains a famous anecdote.

The Opera Stories

歌劇故事

Turandot · 杜蘭朵公主
Carmen · 卡門
Aida · 阿伊達

WORDS
800

Adaptor　Louise Benette, David Hwang
Illustrator　Ludmila Pipchenko

MP3

Let's Enjoy Masterpieces!

All the beautiful fairy tales and masterpieces that you have encountered during your childhood remain as warm memories in your adulthood. This time, let's indulge in the world of masterpieces through English. You can enjoy the depth and beauty of original works, which you can't enjoy through Chinese translations.

The stories are easy for you to understand because of your familiarity with them. When you enjoy reading, your ability to understand English will also rapidly improve.

This series of **Let's Enjoy Masterpieces** is a special reading comprehension booster program, devised to improve reading comprehension for beginners whose command of English is not satisfactory, or who are elementary, middle, and high school students. With this program, you can enjoy reading masterpieces in English with fun and efficiency.

This carefully planned program is composed of 5 levels, from the beginner level of 350 words to the intermediate and advanced levels of 1,000 words. With this program's level-by-level system, you are able to read famous texts in English and to savor the true pleasure of the world's language.

卡門 Opera *Carmen*

Based on the story by the French playwright Merimee, the opera *Carmen* was composed by Bizet, one of the great French composers (1838–1875) in 1875.

Don Jose, a brigadier of the Spanish army stationed in Seville, is a naive young man who has his fiancee and sick mother waiting for him at home.

One day, infatuated by the charms of Carmen, a Gypsy woman working at a cigarette factory, Don Jose abandons his promising career and his fiancee. However, he soon realizes that Carmen has transferred her affections to a bullfighter Escamillo. In a fury of despair, Don Jose stabs Carmen to death in the arena.

The opera *Carmen* was received with harsh criticism when it premiered in 1875 in Paris. The failure was attributed to the fact that the opera didn't appeal to the taste of Parisian aristocrats because it was too risque and vulgar. However, after Bizet's death, when the work was performed again, it received acclaim. Since then, *Carmen* has become one of the most popular operas in the world.

阿伊達 Opera *Aida*

The opera *Aida* is one of the best works of Giuseppe Verdi (1813–1901), a great Italian composer of *Rigoletto* and *La Traviata*.

The opera was commissioned by the Egyptian government for the opening of the Cairo Opera House, in celebration with the opening of the Suez Canal in the fall of 1869.

Aida was first presented for the inauguration of Cairo's new opera house in 1871. Although *Aida* was composed for celebration, the story is a sad love story.

The young Egyptian general, Radames, falls in love with Aida, an Ethiopian princess, who is now a slave to the Egyptian princess, Amneris. Aida loves Radames. However, she is torn between her love of Radames and the love of her homeland, and she suffers from the difference in social status between Radames and herself.

Meanwhile, Amneris, in love with Radames, learns that Radames is in love with Aida. Jealous of Radames's love for Aida, Amneris plots to hinder their love, and eventually, the star-crossed lovers die together.

The opera *Aida* has an ancient Egyptian setting and is considered as one of the grand operas. The scenes of *Aida* are exotic and splendid because of the ancestor worship rites and dances.

In *Aida*, Giuseppe Verdi built a plot as magnificent as life itself, in which universal human emotions, such as love and hate and hope and death, are underscored and transcend time and space. The opera has achieved a reputation of perfectly weaving the various elaborate elements of drama into a majestic story.

HOW TO USE THIS BOOK
本書使用說明

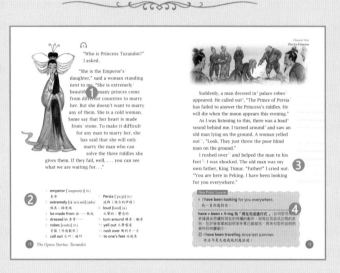

1 Original English texts

It is easy to understand the meaning of the text, because the text is rewritten according to the levels of the readers.

2 Explanation of the vocabulary

The words and expressions that include vocabulary above the elementary level are clearly defined.

3 Response notes

Spaces are included in the book so you can take notes about what you don't understand or what you want to remember.

4 One point lesson

In-depth analyses of major grammar points and expressions help you to understand sentences with difficult grammar.

∩ *Audio Recording*

In the audio recording, native speakers narrate the texts in standard American English. By combining the written words and the audio recording, you can listen to English with great ease.

Audio books have been popular in Britain and America for many decades. They allow the listener to experience the proper word pronunciation and sentence intonation that add important meaning and drama to spoken English. Students will benefit from listening to the recording twenty or more times.

After you are familiar with the text and recording, listen once more with your eyes closed to check your listening comprehension. Finally, after you can listen with your eyes closed and understand every word and every sentence, you are then ready to mimic the native speaker.

Then you should make a recording by reading the text yourself. Then play both recordings to compare your oral skills with those of a native speaker.

CONTENTS

Turandot

杜蘭朵公主

Calaf

My name is Calaf. I was born the Prince of Tartary. I am an old man now, but when I was young I experienced a great challenge. I lost a friend, but I changed the life of a very special person. Do you like riddles? I do.

Princess Turandot

My name is Princess Turandot. Many men ask for my hand, but I refuse to marry them. I think it is important to honor our ancestors, don't you? If you wish to marry me, you must be very clever or else you will pay the price!

King Timur

My name is King Timur. I lost my country in war and my sight while fleeing. I am searching for my son, Calaf. We were separated following the war.

Luckily I have Liu, my servant, to guide me. What would I do without her?

Liu

My name is Liu. I am King Timur's servant. After the war I took care of the King. It is my duty to look after the King and his family. I am very fond of Calaf, and I hope we can find him soon.

Chapter One

The Ice Princess

My life has been full of adventure[1]. Now that I am very old, telling stories is all I can do. My name is Calaf. I was born the Prince of Tartary.

After a very long and terrible war, my father, King Timur, and I were forced to[2] escape from[3] my country. I didn't know what happened[4] to my father but now I was in Peking[5].

1. **adventure** [əd'vent∫ə(r)] (n.)
   冒險;經歷
2. **be forced to** 被迫……
3. **escape from** 從……逃脫
4. **what happened to**
   發生……
5. **Peking** [pekɪŋ] (n.)
   北京的舊譯名
6. **square** [skwer] (n.)
   (方形)廣場
7. **imperial** [ɪm'pɪriəl] (a.)
   帝國的;皇帝的
8. **must have + p.p.**
   必定已經(對過去已發生事情的推測)
9. **be to** 即將發生……

I would never forget the evening I arrived in this great city. Many people had gathered in the square[6] in front of the Imperial[7] Palace. It was really amazing. There must have been[8] thousands of people there.

I thought that something very exciting was to[9] occur[10], so I asked, "What's happening?"

One person in the crowd[11] replied, "A man will be killed soon. He had come to try to marry Princess Turandot. He had to solve[12] the Princess's riddles[13] first before he could marry her, but he failed. Now they will cut off his head."

---

10. **occur** [əˋkɜːr] (v.) 發生
11. **crowd** [kraʊd] (n.) 人群
12. **solve** [sɑːlv] (v.) 解開
13. **riddle** [ˋrɪdl] (n.) 謎；謎語

🎧

"Who is Princess Turandot?" I asked.

"She is the Emperor's[1] daughter," said a woman standing next to me. "She is extremely[2] beautiful. So many princes come from different countries to marry her. But she doesn't want to marry any of them. She is a cold woman. Some say that her heart is made from[3] stone. To make it difficult for any man to marry her, she has said that she will only marry the man who can solve the three riddles she gives them. If they fail, well, . . . you can see what we are waiting for. . ."

1. **emperor** [ˈempərə(r)] (n.)
   皇帝
2. **extremely** [ɪkˈstriːmli] (adv.)
   極其；極度地
3. **be made from** 由⋯⋯做成
4. **dressed in** 身穿⋯⋯
5. **robes** [roʊbz] (n.)
   官服（作複數形）
6. **call out** 大叫；喊叫
7. **Persia** [ˈpɜːʒə] (n.)
   波斯（現今的伊朗）
8. **loud** [laʊd] (a.)
   大聲的；響亮的
9. **turn around** 轉身；翻身
10. **yell out** 大聲嚷道
11. **rush over** 衝到另一方
12. **to one's feet** 站起來

Suddenly, a man dressed in[4] palace robes[5] appeared. He called out[6], "The Prince of Persia[7] has failed to answer the Princess's riddles. He will die when the moon appears this evening."

As I was listening to this, there was a loud[8] sound behind me. I turned around[9] and saw an old man lying on the ground. A woman yelled out[10], "Look. They just threw the poor blind man on the ground."

I rushed over[11] and helped the man to his feet[12]. I was shocked. The old man was my own father, King Timur. "Father!" I cried out. "You are here in Peking. I have been looking for you everywhere."

One Point Lesson

◆ **I have been looking** for you everywhere.
我一直到處找你。

---

have + been + V-ing 為「**現在完成進行式**」：此句型可用於表達過去持續到現在的持續的動作，與現在完成式之間的差別，在於後者單純說明某件事已經做完，而本句型所說明的事件仍持續進行。

e.g. **I have been traveling** since last summer.
從去年夏天起我就到處旅遊。

I looked up[1] and saw another person standing by[2]. It was Liu. She was a very faithful[3] servant[4] and friend to my father. "Liu! You are here too."

"She has been wonderful," said my father. "She has been my eyes ever since I couldn't see and has given me so much help. If she had not been with me, I would have been dead."

Liu was looking down at her feet.

"Liu! I'm most grateful[5] to you for looking after[6] my father. You didn't have to do this. Why have you given so much to me and my family?" I asked her.

1. **look up** 往上看
2. **stand by** 站在旁邊
3. **faithful** [ˋfeɪθfəl] (a.) 忠誠的；忠實的
4. **servant** [ˋsɜ:rvənt] (n.) 僕人
5. **grateful** [ˋgreɪtfəl] (a.) 感激的；感謝的
6. **look after** 照顧
7. **used to + v.** 過去一向
8. **interrupt** [ˌɪntəˋrʌpt] (v.) 打斷；阻礙
9. **gong** [gɔ:ŋ] (n.) 鑼
10. **executioner** [ˌeksɪˋkju:ʃənə(r)] (n.) 劊子手
11. **sharpen** [ˋʃɑːrpən] (v.) 磨利；削尖
12. **ax** [æks] (n.) 斧頭
13. **cold-hearted** [ˌkoʊldˋhɑːrtɪd] (a.) 無情的；鐵石心腸的

"A long time ago in the palace, you used to smile[7] at me," she said but her words were interrupted[8] by a loud gong[9].

Many men entered the square. They carried a large stone to the middle of the square. The stone was for the executioner[10] to sharpen[11] his ax[12] on.

"Cut off his head when the moon appears!" people shouted. I was quite shocked by the people. It seemed they enjoyed watching people die.

"These people are like animals," I thought. "How can this Princess Turandot kill so many men. She really is a cold-hearted[13] woman."

Everyone continued[1] calling for[2] the death of the poor man, but they became very quiet when the Princess appeared.

The Princess was wearing a long white robe. From a distance[3], it looked like ice. She had beautiful black hair, which was so long that it almost reached[4] the floor. Her face was perfect and her lips were red like roses.

She opened those beautiful lips and ordered, "Guards[5]! Take him away to cut off his head!"

1. **continue** [kən`tɪnjuː] (v.) 繼續
2. **call for** 要求
3. **from a distance** 從遠處
4. **reach** [riːtʃ] (v.) 抵達
5. **guard** [ɡɑːrd] (n.) 衛兵

6. **drag** [dræg] (v.) 拉；拖 (drag-dragged-dragged)
7. **spell** [spel] (n.) 咒語
8. **cast on** 投射；下（咒）(cast-cast-cast)
9. **desire** [dɪ`zaɪə(r)] (n.) 渴望
10. **beat** [biːt] (v.) 跳動

The poor prince was dragged[6] away to his death. It was such a terrible night but I could not think of the poor man anymore.

It was like a spell[7] had been cast on[8] me. All I could think of was the Princess. I couldn't take my eyes off of her. I was filled with desire[9] and love for her. For a moment, my heart even stopped beating[10]!

5

Then, I did something which would change my life forever. I said in a very loud voice, "I have come here to make the Princess my bride. I will solve her riddles and she will marry me."

"No, no! They will cut your head off. I can't bear¹ to think of that," Liu cried.

"This means² I will lose you again. Please don't do this," Father begged³ me.

But I didn't listen to them. I walked toward a very large gong in the square. Anyone who wanted to marry the Princess had to hit the gong three times.

1. **bear** [ber] (v.) 忍受
   (bear-bore-borne)
2. **mean** [miːn] (v.) 意味
   (mean-meant-meant)
3. **beg** [beg] (v.) 懇求
4. **walk up to** 往前走向⋯⋯
5. **race** [reɪs] (v.) 快速前進
6. **grand** [grænd] (a.)
   高階的
7. **chancellor** [ˋtʃænsələ(r)]
   (n.) 大臣；閣員
8. **chief** [tʃiːf] (a.) 階級最高的
9. **marshal** [ˋmɑːrʃəl] (n.)
   元帥；高級將領

As I walked up[4] to the gong, three men raced[5] in front of me and stopped me.

One said, "I am Ping, the Grand[6] Chancellor[7]." The second said, "I am Pong, the Chief[8] Cook." The third said, "I am Pang, the Marshal[9]."

"Do not do this!" they all cried out.

Pang said, "Look in the sky! Can't you see the ghosts[10] of the dead flying around this great city? They are the men who died for the Princess's love."

Ping said, "There are so many pretty women. Go and find another pretty girl."

I just said, "No!" and walked past[11] them. I struck[12] the gong three times.

10. **ghost** [goʊst] (n.) 鬼魂；幽靈
11. **past** [pæst] (prep.) 經過
12. **strike** [straɪk] (v.) 擊打

The whole[1] crowd watched me hit the gong and then I could hear them whisper[2], "He will never solve the riddles."

The three men were also talking among themselves. "There have already been thirteen deaths this year. This city is filled with blood."

Even though everyone thought I would die, I would not change my mind[3]. I wanted to marry the Princess. Soon, two guards came out and took me inside the Palace.

After a few moments, a group of wise men[4] walked in with large documents[5]. I guessed[6] they contained[7] the Princess's riddles.

After the wise men, came some other men. They were carrying[8] red and white lanterns[9]. Red was for a wedding and white was for a funeral[10].

1. **whole** [houl] (a.) 全部的
2. **whisper** [ˈwɪspə(r)] (v.) 低語；私語
3. **mind** [maɪnd] (n.) 心意
4. **wise man** 智者
5. **document** [ˈdɑːkjumənt] (n.) 公文；文件
6. **guess** [ges] (v.) 猜測
7. **contain** [kənˈteɪn] (v.) 包含
8. **carry** [ˈkæri] (v.) 提；帶著
9. **lantern** [ˈlæntərn] (n.) 燈籠
10. **funeral** [ˈfjuːnərəl] (n.) 葬禮
11. **twice** [twaɪs] (adv.) 兩次
12. **let me + v.** 允許；讓我

Finally, the Emperor appeared. He did not look like a happy man.

He looked at me and said, "Please do not do this. Don't try to answer my daughter's riddles. You can leave now before she comes."

"No," I replied. "I will try to answer."

The Emperor asked me twice[11] more, and I answered each time, " Let me try[12]."

A Choose the correct answer.

1 If your friend is _____, you can trust him.

(a) faithful   (b) kind

(c) generous   (d) hardworking

2 If you _____ something, it means you strongly want to have it.

(a) like   (b) desire

(c) hate   (d) miss

3 On the wedding day, the _____ wears a white dress.

(a) best man   (b) bridegroom

(c) husband   (d) bride

B Choose the word from the list that best matches the definition.

fail interrupt arrive force whisper solve

1 To speak in a very quiet voice: _____

2 To make someone do something against his / her will: _____

3 To reach one's destination: _____

4 To find the answer to something: _____

5 To be unsuccessful at something: _____

6 To break in on someone's speech or action: _____

C Choose the correct answer.

❶ Why did Calaf come to Peking?

(a) To marry the Princess Turandot.

(b) Because of the war in his country.

(c) Because he liked adventures very much.

❷ Why do the people call Turandot the ice princess?

(a) Because she looks like ice in her white robe.

(b) Because she is a cold-hearted woman.

(c) Because everybody hated her.

D True or False.

❶ Anyone who wanted to marry the princess Turandot, had to solve her riddles first. T F

❷ Liu came to Peking with the King Timur to meet Calaf. T F

❸ Calaf fell in love with Turandot when he first saw her. T F

❹ Ping, Pong, and Pang all believed that Calaf could solve the riddles. T F

❺ If you want to challenge the princess's riddles, you should call her name loudly three times. T F

The Forbidden City

The Peking described in the opera *Turandot* does not exist anymore. Giacomo Puccini, the Italian composer of this opera, never visited China. Instead, he was inspired by Marco Polo's travels.

Marco Polo journeyed to China 1,000 years ago and wrote about a fantastic walled city on a hill in the center of the Chinese capital of Peking. This was the Forbidden City.

It was named this because only royalty and their servants could enter the gates. When Princess Turnadot speaks to the public, she comes to the main gate.

In Marco Polo's time, Peking's streets were wide and straight. He wrote that the city looked like a checkerboard, with neat square blocks of old mansions and fine inns.

These days, the walls and buildings of the Forbidden City still stand, but the gates are wide open to tourists from all over the world. Turandot and all Chinese royalty may be gone, but the city they lived in still stands.

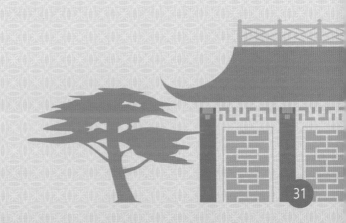

Chapter Two

🎧 Three Riddles

A few moments later, the Princess appeared. She was very beautiful and elegant[1]. She stood like a tall white candle. She started to speak and I felt my heart[2] leap out[3] from my chest[4].

"I am taking revenge[5] for the death of my ancestor[6], Princess Lou Ling. A thousand years ago, a foreign king came to her in this place, ravished[7] and murdered[8] her. To honor[9] her memory, I have vowed[10] to never allow[11] any man to touch me. There are three riddles for you but only one death," she said.

I replied, "There are three riddles but only one life."

The Opera Stories: Turandot

1. **elegant** [ˋɛlɪgənt] (a.)
   端莊的；優雅的
2. **heart** [hɑːrt] (n.) 心臟
3. **leap out** 跳出來
4. **chest** [tʃɛst] (n.) 胸膛
5. **take revenge** 復仇

6. **ancestor** [ˋænsɛstə(r)] (n.) 祖先
7. **ravish** [ˋrævɪʃ] (v.) 強奪
8. **murder** [ˋmɜːrdə(r)] (v.) 謀殺
9. **honor** [ˋɑːnər] (v.) 致敬
10. **vow** [vaʊ] (v.) 發誓
11. **allow** [ɑˋlaʊ] (v.) 容許

She began to ask me the first riddle. "What is the phantom[1] born every night that dies in the dawn[2] but lives in the hearts of humans?"

I thought carefully about the question and answered, "Hope."

She looked very uncomfortable[3] after I answered but she continued to ask the second riddle.

"What warms[4] like a fire, boils[5] in a fever[7], becomes cold in death, but glows[8] like a sunset and flies into passion[9] in victory?"

Once more, I thought carefully about the question and answered, "Blood."

1. **phantom** [ˋfæntəm] (n.)
   幻影；幻覺
2. **dawn** [dɔːn] (n.) 黎明
3. **uncomfortable**
   [ʌnˋkʌmfərtəbəl] (a.)
   不自在的；不安的

4. **warm** [wɔːrm] (v.) 使暖和
5. **boil** [bɔɪl] (v.) 沸騰；激昂
6. **fever** [ˋfiːvə(r)] (n.)
   狂熱；興奮
7. **glow** [ɡloʊ] (v.) 發光
8. **fly into** 飛到……裡

Now Turandot looked at me in anger[10]. Her eyes looked as cold as ice. She asked the final question. "What is the ice that sets you on fire[11]? What consumes[12] you and yet freezes[13] even harder?"

The crowd in the square stood silent and listened. This time I thought even longer about the question.

"Turandot," I said at last. Finally, I said, "Turandot. You are like ice but my passion for you burns[14] inside me. You are what consumes my thoughts and feelings[15]."

9. **passion** [ˋpæʃən] (n.) 熱情
10. **in anger** 盛怒
11. **set A on fire** 使某物燃燒
12. **consume** [kənˋsjuːm] (v.) 消耗

13. **freeze** [friːz] (v.) 凍結
    (freeze-froze-frozen)
14. **burn** [bɜːrn] (v.) 燃燒
15. **feeling** [ˋfiːlɪŋ] (n.) 感情；感覺

The wise men standing in the square in that magnificent[1] palace shook their heads[2] in amazement[3]. I had answered the three riddles correctly[4]. Turandot looked stunned[5] for a few moments.

Then, she threw herself at[6] her father's feet and begged, "Please do not make me marry him. Please, father!"

But her father replied, "He has answered all of the questions correctly. We promised that whoever[7] answers the questions correctly, will marry you. You must!"

Turandot now stood and turned to look at me. "Do you really want a wife who marries you unwillingly[8]?" she asked.

"No, I do not," I replied. "So, if you can find out[9] my name before dawn tomorrow, I will not force you to marry me and I will die happily at your hands[10].

---

1. **magnificent** [mæg`nɪfɪsənt] (a.) 壯麗宏偉的
2. **shake head** 搖頭
3. **in amazement** 詫異地
4. **correctly** [kə`rektli] (adv.) 正確地
5. **stunned** [stʌnd] (a.) 吃驚的
6. **throw oneself at** 猛烈前進
7. **whoever** [hu:`evə(r)] (pron.) 無論誰
8. **unwillingly** [ʌn`wɪlɪŋli] (adv.) 不情願地；勉強地

This pleased[11] Turandot very much. She smiled in her own evil[12] way and said, "Wonderful. No one will sleep tonight until I learn[13] your name. Tomorrow, you will lose your head. I will give a reward[14] to the person who finds out your name."

That night, no one in the city could sleep. I waited in the palace garden for the sun to rise. Ping, Pong, and Pang came to see me. Again they begged, "The Princess will find out your name. Just please leave in peace before she kills you."

Suddenly, I heard a noise inside the courtyard[15]. I rushed in to see some guards dragging my father and Liu into the courtyard.

One of the guards said, "These people spoke to him yesterday. They know who he is."

I shouted out, "No, they don't. Until yesterday, they were complete[16] strangers to me."

---

9. **find out** 找出；發現

10. **die at one's hands** 死在……手中

11. **please** [pliːz] (v.) 使高興；使滿意

12. **evil** [ˋiːvəl] (a.) 邪惡的

13. **learn** [lɜːrn] (v.) 得知；獲悉

14. **reward** [rɪˋwɔːrd] (n.) 獎賞；報償

15. **courtyard** [ˋkɔːrtjɑːrd] (n.) 庭院

16. **complete** [kəmˋpliːt] (a.) 完全的；絕對的

As soon as Turandot arrived, the guards started beating[1] my father. Liu cried out, "Please do not hurt[2] him. He is only an old man. Only I can tell you what you want to know."

I tried to run to Liu to stop her from[3] speaking but some guards stopped me.

Turandot ordered, "Take her and torture[4] her until she tells you his name."

"I will never tell you," Liu screamed[5]. "I will die before I tell you his name."

I was so stunned by Liu's devotion[6] to my father and myself, and even Turandot asked her, "Why do you care so much about[7] him? Why are you so willing to[8] sacrifice yourself for[9] this man?"

1. **beat** [biːt] (v.) 重擊;打
2. **hurt** [hɜːrt] (v.) 傷害
3. **stop A from** 阻止 A 做……
4. **torture** [ˋtɔːrtʃə(r)] (v.)
   折磨;拷打
5. **scream** [skriːm] (v.) 尖叫
6. **devotion** [dɪˋvoʊʃən] (n.)
   忠誠;奉獻
7. **care about** 關心;在乎
8. **willing to** 願意;樂意
9. **sacrifice for . . .**
   為……犧牲
10. **courage** [ˋkɜːrɪdʒ] (n.)
    勇氣;膽量
11. **be made of** 由……做成
12. **grab** [ɡræb] (v.) 奪取;抓
    (grab-grabbed-grabbed)
13. **dagger** [ˋdæɡə(r)] (n.)
    匕首;短劍
14. **stab** [stæb] (v.) 刺向;刺傷

Liu answered, "Love gives me courage[10]. Your heart is made of[11] ice but it will be warmed by the love he can give."

Liu jumped forward and grabbed[12] one of the guard's daggers[13] and stabbed[14] herself in the heart. No one could have stopped Liu because it all happened so quickly. She fell to the ground in front of my feet and died.

I felt such emotion[1] for poor Liu. She had given her life to save[2] mine. I became very angry now.

I turned to Turandot and said, "You are the Princess of Death. Wherever you go, death follows[3] you."

Turandot looked at me and said, "No. I am the Daughter of Heaven and my spirit[4] flies in the heavens, far above yours."

"Perhaps your spirit may but you are on this earth[5] with me. So you are no better than[6] the rest[7] of us."

I walked toward her and tore[8] her veil[9] away. I took her in my arms and placed[10] my lips on hers. At first she struggled[11] like a wild animal but the warmth[12] of my kiss finally reached her frozen[13] heart. She broke down into tears[14].

"The love in my kiss has warmed your heart. You will no longer[15] be the Ice Princess," I told her.

1. **emotion** [ɪˋmouʃən] (n.) 激動
2. **save** [seɪv] (v.) 拯救
3. **follow** [ˋfɑːlou] (v.) 跟隨
4. **spirit** [ˋspɪrɪt] (n.) 心靈
5. **earth** [ɜːrθ] (n.) 俗世
6. **no better than** 和……一樣
7. **rest** [rest] (n.) 其餘（的人）
8. **tear** [ter] (v.) 撕開
   (tear-tore-torn)
9. **veil** [veɪl] (n.) 面紗
10. **place** [pleɪs] (v.) 放置
11. **struggle** [ˋstrʌgəl] (v.)
    掙扎；對抗
12. **warmth** [wɔːrmθ] (n.) 溫暖
13. **frozen** [ˋfrouzən] (a.)
    結冰的；無情的
14. **break down into tears**
    崩潰流淚
15. **no longer** 不再

"As soon as[1] I saw you I knew that you would make my life difficult," the princess said. "Go. I do not want to know your name. It can stay[2] a mystery[3]."

I replied, "I am the victor[4] now and I do not care[5] whether I live or die. My name is Calaf, Prince of Tartary."

Later, after the sun had risen, the King sat on his throne[6]. Turandot and I were standing together in front of him.

1. **as soon as**
   一……，就……
2. **stay** [steɪ] (v.) 保持

3. **mystery** [`mɪstri] (n.)
   謎；神秘的事物
4. **victor** [`vɪktə(r)] (n.) 勝利者
5. **care** [ker] (v.) 在乎

The Emperor spoke to Turandot first. "Turandot. Have you discovered[7] the name of this man?"

"Yes, I have, Father. His name is Love," she replied. Then, she smiled in a way no one had ever seen before. The smile was not of hate[8] or evil but of love.

Ping, Pong, and Pang nodded[9] approvingly[10] and the Emperor looked happy.

Turandot became my wife and we have lived very happily for many years. It is wonderful to grow old[11] with the person you love.

6. **throne** [θroʊn] (n.) 王座
7. **discover** [dɪˈskʌvə(r)] (v.) 發現
8. **hate** [heɪt] (v.) 仇恨
9. **nod** [nɑːd] (v.) 點頭
10. **approvingly** [əˈpruːvɪŋli] (adv.) 贊成地
11. **grow old** 變老

A Read the four sentences and write down who said each sentence.

Turandot

Calaf

Liu

Ping, Pong, Pang

❶ Please do not hurt him. He is only an old man. _____

❷ Why are you so willing to sacrifice yourself for this man? _____

❸ You are like ice but my passion for you burns inside me. _____

❹ Just please leave in peace before she kills you. _____

B Correct the mistakes.

❶ I have promised never allow any man to touch me.

⇨ _____

❷ I am thinking of go to Greece for my next vacation.

⇨ _____

❸ I am look forward your birthday party next week.

⇨ _____

Carmen

卡門

Before You Read

Carmen

My name is Carmen. I am a Gypsy. I love life and I love to be free. Men easily fall under my spell. They are such fools. No man will ever choose me. I will always decide who I love. I believe in destiny. Don't you?

Don Jose

My name is Don Jose. I am a soldier. The best thing about being a soldier is the changing of guards at noon. I like looking at the pretty factory workers in the square. I wonder if I will ever have a chance to meet one of them.

Micaela

My name is Micaela. I come from the country. I am Don Jose's girl. He is a good man, but I often catch him looking at other women. This worries me.

Escamillo

My name is Escamillo. I am a bullfighter. I usually fight on Sundays in front of large crowds. Women like to watch me fight because I am so attractive in my uniform.

Chapter One

The Gypsy[1] and the Soldier[2]

I am from Spain. I do not need to tell you my name[3]. It is not important for this story. The only name you really need to remember is the name, Carmen.

In a small town, there was a man named Jose. He was a soldier and he lived in the army barracks[4], which were on one side of[5] the town square. On the other side, there was a cigarette[6] factory.

1. **Gypsy** [ˋdʒɪpsi] (n.) 吉普賽人
2. **soldier** [ˋsouldʒə(r)] (n.) 軍人；士兵
3. **name** [neɪm] (v.) 命名；以……稱呼
4. **army barrack** 軍營
5. **on a side of** 在……的一邊
6. **cigarette** [ˋsɪɡəret] (n.) 香菸
7. **sweetheart** [ˋswi:tha:rt] (n.) 心上人；情人
8. **captain** [ˋkæptɪn] (n.) 隊長；上尉
9. **guard** [gɑ:rd] (n.) 衛兵；守衛
10. **look for** 尋找

One day, a girl named Micaela went to this town. She came from the country and Jose was her sweetheart[7].

As soon as she arrived at the square, she spoke to the Captain[8] of the Guard[9].

"Excuse me. I'm looking for[10] Don Jose. I've come from his village to bring a letter from his mother," she said.

The man replied, "The guard changes at noon and he will be here then. You can wait until then."

"Thank you," she said.

🎧14

　　While she waited, she heard the sound of a whistle[1]. It came from the cigarette factory. This meant it was lunchtime for the workers. All the women came out of[2] the factory and went to the square to eat their lunches. Carmen was one of those women.

There is no way to describe[3] her. She was a Gypsy girl who entrapped[4] every man with her charm[5].

She was beautiful and magical[6]. She loved passionately[7], but she became bored[8] easily. She would cast aside[9] a man as quickly as she loved him.

She loved her freedom. She always wanted to be the one who did the choosing. She was like a bird that would rather[10] die than be trapped[11] in a cage[12].

She would always say to her friends, "No man will choose me. I will always decide who I love."

1. **whistle** [ˋwɪsəl] (n.)
   笛聲；哨音
2. **out of** 從……
3. **describe** [dɪˋskraɪb] (v.)
   形容；描述
4. **entrap** [ɪnˋtræp] (v.)
   使入陷阱
5. **charm** [tʃɑːrm] (n.) 魅力
6. **magical** [ˋmædʒɪkəl] (a.)
   神秘的；迷人的
7. **passionately** [ˋpæʃənətli]
   (adv.) 熱情地
8. **bore** [bɔː(r)] (v.) 厭煩
9. **cast aside** 拋棄
10. **rather** [ˋræðə(r)] (adv.)
    寧可；寧願
11. **trap** [træp] (v.) 誘入圈套
12. **cage** [keɪdʒ] (n.) 籠

While the women were eating their meals[1], the change of guard took place[2].

Many soldiers marched[3] into the square. When they saw Carmen, they all behaved[4] differently. Each man flirted[5] with her and tried to get her attention[6]. But she laughed[7] at their childish[8] efforts[9].

"Why are you all trying so hard? I like a man who is hard to get. Love is never simple. It shows itself just when you are not expecting it."

Don Jose was also there in the square. He came under her spell[10] immediately[11]. He couldn't take his eyes off her. She suddenly turned around and saw him.

1. **meal** [miːl] (n.) 一餐
2. **take place** 發生；舉行
3. **march** [mɑːrtʃ] (v.) 行進；前進
4. **behave** [bɪˈheɪv] (v.) 表現
5. **flirt** [flɜːrt] (v.) 調情
6. **attention** [əˈtenʃən] (n.) 注意力
7. **laugh at** 嘲笑
8. **childish** [ˈtʃaɪldɪʃ] (a.) 幼稚的
9. **effort** [ˈefərt] (n.) 努力；盡力
10. **under a spell** 被迷惑
11. **immediately** [ɪˈmiːdiətli] (adv.) 即刻地
12. **blow** [blou] (v.) 吹響
13. **directly** [dəˈrektli] (adv.) 直接地
14. **walk up to** 走上前
15. **sweetly** [ˈswiːtli] (adv.) 甜蜜地；溫柔地

The Opera Stories: Carmen

Just at that moment the whistle of the cigarette factory blew[12] again. Carmen called to her friends, "Frasquita! Mercedes! We have to go back to work."

But Carmen did not directly[13] go to the factory. She walked up to[14] Don Jose. From her lovely hair, she pulled a red rose and threw it down at his feet and smiled sweetly[15].

At the time this story took place, many people believed in[1] fate[2]. They believed that everything that happened was controlled[3] by destiny[4].

Don Jose knew that if he picked up[5] the rose, he would be trapped forever by her. If that happened, Carmen could do whatever[6] she wanted with his heart.

They remained[7] looking at each other. After a long silence[8], he bent[9] down and picked up the rose. Now he was hers. He was bewitched[11], and could do nothing but wait for destiny to show him his future happiness.

1. **believe in** 相信
2. **fate** [feɪt] (n.) 命運
3. **control** [kən`troʊl] (v.) 支配；控制
4. **destiny** [`dɛstəni] (n.) 命運
5. **pick up** 拾起
6. **whatever** [wɑːt`ɛvə(r)] (pron.) 任何……的事物
7. **remain** [rɪ`meɪn] (v.) 保持
8. **silence** [`saɪləns] (n.) 寂靜；無聲
9. **bend** [bɛnd] (v.) 彎腰；彎身 (bend-bent-bent)
10. **bewitch** [bɪ`wɪtʃ] (v.) 蠱惑；著迷
11. **concentrate on** 專心於
12. **no doubt** 無疑地
13. **disappointed** [dɪsə`pɔɪntɪd] (a.) 失望的；沮喪的

Just after all the women had left, Micaela entered the square. Don Jose was very surprised and pleased to see her. He was also very happy to receive the letter from his mother. But he could not concentrate on[11] Micaela or the letter. His mind and heart were in another place.

Micaela left, no doubt[12] feeling disappointed[13] that Don Jose did not want to talk longer to her. After she left, he almost never thought of her again.

One day, a fight broke out[1] in the factory, and Carmen wounded[2] another woman. No one even knew how the fight started. Anyway, Carmen was arrested[3]. A captain in the army, Zuniga, told Don Jose that he was in charge of[4] the group of men to take her to prison[5].

When Carmen saw Don Jose, she smiled sweetly at him.

"It is destiny for us to be together. Let me go[6] free when we go across the bridge. Then, I'll meet you at Lilla Pastia's tavern. I promise I will love only you."

"I cannot," replied Don Jose. "I have to take you to prison."

"You have to let me go because your heart is in my power[7]. You picked up the rose. It's a magic flower that binds[8] us together. Can't you feel it?" she said.

Don Jose had a difficult time with this. But she was right. He had to let her go. As she ran off[9], she said, "Lilla Pastia's tavern! Don't forget!"

1. **break out** 爆發
   (break-broke-broken)
2. **wound** [wu:nd] (v.)
   打傷；傷害
3. **arrest** [əˋrest] (v.) 逮捕
4. **in charge of** 負責管理
5. **prison** [ˋprɪzən] (n.) 監獄
6. **let go** 釋放
7. **in one's power** 被某人控制
8. **bind** [baɪnd] (v.) 綁
   (bind-bound-bound)
9. **run off** 逃走

When Zuniga found out[1] Carmen had escaped, he was furious[2].

"You are such an idiot[3]! You let her escape and now you have to be punished[4]. Lock[5] him away in prison!"

It was well-known[6] that Zuniga loved Carmen too. In fact, he was relieved[7] to have his rival[8] taken away[9] to prison. Poor Don Jose just wondered[10] how long it would be before he saw Carmen again.

Many months passed by[11] and one night in Lilla Pastia's tavern, Carmen was with her friends Frasquita and Mercedes. They were drinking wine and talking to some smugglers[12].

Zuniga was also there. He had begged Carmen to forget Don Jose many times.

"He has forgotten you for sure[13]," he told her. "You think he will come here for you but he won't. He was released[14] from prison today and he hasn't come."

Carmen said, "He loves me, so he will come. I promised I would wait. I must keep my promise[15]."

1. **find out** 發現
2. **furious** [ˋfjuəriəs] (a.) 狂怒的
3. **idiot** [ˋɪdiət] (n.) 白癡
4. **punish** [ˋpʌnɪʃ] (v.) 懲罰
5. **lock** [lɑːk] (v.) 鎖住
6. **well-known** (a.)
   出名的；眾所周知的
7. **relieved** [rɪˋliːvd] (a.) 放心的
8. **rival** [ˋraɪvəl] (n.)
   對手；競爭者
9. **take away** 帶走
10. **wonder** [ˋwʌndə(r)] (v.)
    納悶；想知道
11. **pass by** 過去
12. **smuggler** [ˋsmʌglə(r)] (n.)
    走私者
13. **for sure** 確切地
14. **release** [rɪˋliːs] (v.) 釋放
15. **keep one's promise**
    信守承諾

Just then, Frasquita said, "Listen. It is
Escamillo's procession[1]. They are going to
Seville. Let's go and meet him."

The Opera Stories: Carmen

Escamillo was a bullfighter[2]. He was always very well-dressed in a tight[3] satin[4] suit[5], and so many girls thought he was very handsome.

He came into the tavern and saw Carmen. "What is your name?" he asked.

"I am Carmen," she said.

"I'll use your name as a charm[6] to keep me safe when I fight the bulls[7]." Everyone could see that Carmen was looking at him very passionately.

It was fate that took Escamillo to the tavern. This story would end very differently[8] if he had gone to a different place that night.

1. **procession** [prə`seʃən] (n.) 行列；隊伍
2. **bullfighter** [`bulfaɪtər] (n.) 鬥牛士
3. **tight** [taɪt] (a.) 緊身的
4. **satin** [`sætɪn] (n.) 緞
5. **suit** [suːt] (n.) 套裝
6. **charm** [tʃɑːrm] (n.) 護身符
7. **bull** [bul] (n.) 公牛
8. **differently** [`dɪfrəntli] (adv.) 不同地

After Escamillo had left, Don Jose walked through the door. Carmen ran to him and he said, "Carmen, my love! You are here just as you promised." Then, they danced together until the sun rose[1].

"I must go now," he said. "It is daylight[2] and I must return to the barracks."

"Don't go back," she begged. "Stay with me and let's join[3] the smugglers. We can live in the mountains and be free."

"I cannot desert[4] my army," he said. Carmen stepped back[5]. "And I cannot love a coward[6]. If you will not risk[7] anything for me, then you do not love me."

It seemed as if she wanted a reason[8] for him to leave her, so she could run to Escamillo.

1. **rise** [raɪz] (v.) 升起；上升
2. **daylight** [`deɪlaɪt] (n.) 黎明；白晝
3. **join** [dʒɔɪn] (v.) 參加
4. **desert** [dɪ`zɜːrt] (v.) 擅離職守
5. **step back** 往後退
6. **coward** [`kaʊərd] (n.) 懦夫
7. **risk** [rɪsk] (n.) 風險
8. **reason** [`riːzən] (n.) 理由

"Come with us," Carmen asked him again.

"I love you and so I will come with you," he said.

So Don Jose went to join the smugglers in the mountains with Carmen.

A True or False.

1 Carmen was working in the cigarette factory. T F

2 When Don Jose saw Carmen for the first time, he couldn't take his eyes from her. T F

3 When Carmen was arrested, Don Jose took her to prison. T F

4 Carmen believed Don Jose would come to the tavern. T F

5 Escamillo was a smuggler, and he loved Carmen. T F

B Choose the correct answer.

1 Why did Micaela go to see Don Jose in the square?

(a) To tell him she loved him.

(b) To deliver a letter from his mother to him.

(c) To tell him she was getting married.

2 Why did Don Jose hesitate to pick up the rose Carmen threw at his feet?

(a) Because he did not want to be trapped by her.

(b) Because he didn't know if he liked her.

(c) Because he was in love with another woman.

❸ Why did Carmen injure another woman?

   (a) Because the other woman wanted to marry Don Jose.

   (b) Because the other woman spat at her.

   (c) Nobody knew why.

C Fill in the blanks with the given words.

| desert | risk | coward | barracks | begged |

"I must go now," he said. "It is daylight and I must return to the **❶** _____."

"Don't go back," she **❷** _____. "Stay with me and let's join the smugglers. We can live in the mountains and be free."

"I cannot **❸** _____ my army," he said. Carmen stepped back.

"And I cannot love a **❹** _____. If you will not **❺** _____ anything for me, then you do not love me."

Gypsies and
Their Lives

Carmen was a Gypsy, so her life seemed wild and adventurous. Modern scientific studies have shown that Gypsies were wanderers who left India 1,000 years ago and entered Europe in the 16th century.

Many Europeans, and even many Gypsies themselves, believed they were from Egypt. This is how they got their name: first they were called Egyptians, then "Gyptians", and finally "Gypsies."

When the Gypsies reached Europe, most of the land was already settled. Gypsies were not Christian like most Europeans. They had darker skin and a different language and culture.

For these reasons, Europeans did not welcome the Gypsies. As a result, the Gypsies usually did not settle in any particular place. There were stories that the Gypsies practiced magic, or were immoral.

Carmen represents this wild, sexual image of the Gypsies. Her lover, the Spanish soldier, cannot control her, so he kills her. Unfortunately, this is what happened many times throughout European history as the Gypsies were punished for their differences.

· Chapter Two ·

[21]

A Very Difficult and Sad Life

Life was very difficult for Don Jose and
Carmen. They had no comfort[1] in their lives.
In the summer, they slept under the stars and
in the winter, they slept in very old dirty
tents[2].

In the beginning, their passion[3] for each other was enough but Carmen quickly became bored.

One day she said, "You should go home. This life is not good for you. Go back to your mother and your little village. The only thing you are good at[4] is marching around in your silly uniform."

"I want to go but I will not. I love you and so I should stay here and be with you. I will never leave you," he replied.

1. **comfort** [ˋkʌmfərt] (n.)
   安逸；舒適
2. **tent** [tent] (n.) 帳篷

3. **passion** [ˋpæʃən] (n.) 熱情
4. **be good at** 善於

"But this life is difficult and you will come to hate me. You may even kill me one day," Carmen said.

Carmen always thought of death. Sometime before, she and her friends had dealt the card[1], while playing as fortune-tellers[2].

Frasquita said, "I am looking for love! I want a young man to love me forever."

Mercedes said, laughing, "I want an old man. I want a rich old man who will die quickly and leave all of his money to me!"

While telling each other's fortunes[3], Carmen picked one card. Then they put the card back[4] and mixed[5] the cards.

1. **deal the card** 發牌
2. **fortune-teller** 算命者
3. **fortune** [ˋfɔːrtʃuːn] (n.) 命運
4. **put back** 放回原處

5. **mix** [mɪks] (v.) 混合
6. **spade** [speɪd] (n.) 黑桃
7. **lie** [laɪ] (v.) 撒謊

She took another card. It was the same card. "It's the two of spades[6]. You picked it twice," cried her friends. That card had only one meaning. It was the Death card.

"So I am going to die. The cards never lie[7]," Carmen said. She knew that death was waiting for her and there was no way she could stop it.

The next day, Micaela arrived in the smugglers' camp [1]. She was looking for [2] Don Jose. But she quickly hid [3] behind a rock because another person also came to the camp at the same time.

It was Escamillo, the bullfighter. As soon as Don Jose saw him, he began shooting [4] at him.

Escamillo shouted out, "I am not the police so stop shooting at me. I have only come for Carmen!"

1. **camp** [kæmp] (n.)
   營地；帳篷
2. **look for** 尋找
3. **hide** [haɪd] (v.) 躲藏
4. **shoot** [ʃuːt] (v.) 射擊
5. **what if** 假使；若是

"What if[5] she will not go with you?" Don Jose asked him.

"I know that she will come. When we first met, she looked at me in a way that she does not look at other men. She has also been with a deserter[6] from the army. That is not good for her. She will come with me," replied Escamillo.

"It's very dangerous[7] to take a Gypsy's woman away from him," Don Jose warned[8] Escamillo.

But Escamillo only laughed and said, "That is true, but you are no Gypsy.
You are a soldier."

6. **deserter** [dɪ`sɜːrtə(r)] (n.) 逃兵

7. **dangerous** [`deɪndʒərəs] (a.) 危險的

8. **warn** [wɔːrn] (v.) 警告

Just then, Carmen and the smugglers returned to[1] the camp. One of the smugglers said to Escamillo, "He will kill you unless[2] you leave right now."

The bullfighter replied, "Alright. I will go. But I want to invite you all to the bullring[3] on Sunday to see me fight."

Escamillo looked directly at Carmen and said, "And those who[4] love me are especially[5] welcome to come and see me." Escamillo then left the camp.

As soon as he had gone, Micaela came out from her hiding place. "I have a message[6] for Don Jose from his mother. His mother is sick and she wants to see him," she said.

1. **return to** 返回到
2. **unless** [ənˋles] (conj.) 除非
3. **bullring** [ˋbʊlrɪŋ] (n.) 鬥牛場
4. **those who** 那些……的人
5. **especially** [ɪˋspeʃəli] (adv.) 特別；尤其
6. **message** [ˋmesɪdʒ] (n.) 口信；消息
7. **leave A to** 讓某人去做
8. **bluntly** [ˋblʌntli] (adv.) 直言不諱地
9. **tremble** [ˋtrembəl] (v.) 發抖

"Don Jose, please come with me!"

Carmen said to Don Jose, "Yes, you should go."

Don Jose turned around and asked, "And what? Leave you to[7] run into the arms of Escamillo?"

Carmen replied very bluntly[8], "Yes! I have no more love for you. We are finished."

Don Jose prepared to leave the camp. Before he left he said to Carmen, "I promise that we will meet again." His voice was trembling[9].

The next events[1] happened a few weeks later. One Sunday, there was a very important bullfight in Seville. The bullring was crowded with[2] spectators[3].

Escamillo arrived for the fight and Carmen came with him. She had never looked better.

This only made Don Jose, who was waiting for her in the crowd, more jealous[4].

Frasquita and Mercedes had seen him.
"Carmen! He is here. You must be careful[5]," they pleaded.

"No, I will go and see him if that's what he wants. I will not run from him."

Carmen went off[6] to look for Don Jose. When she found him, she said, "My friends said that you were here. They are worried you want to kill me."

"I do not want to kill you. I want you to love me again. My life is nothing[7] without you. Please come back to me." he said.

"Remember, I choose who I love. I don't love you anymore. I must go now. The bullfight is over[8]," she said.

Don Jose was becoming angry. "You love him, don't you? Don't deny[9] it!" he snapped[10].

"I will never deny it! I do love him," she said, laughing as she spoke.

---

1. **event** [ɪˋvent] (n.) 事件；大事
2. **be crowded with** 擠滿
3. **spectator** [spekˋteɪtə(r)] (n.) 觀眾
4. **jealous** [ˋdʒeləs] (a.) 嫉妒的
5. **careful** [ˋkerfəl] (a.) 小心的
6. **go off** 離開
7. **nothing** [ˋnʌθɪŋ] (n.) 毫無價值之物
8. **over** [ˋoʊvə(r)] (a.) 結束的
9. **deny** [dɪˋnaɪ] (v.) 否認；否定
10. **snap** [snæp] (v.) 怒罵；吼叫

He tried to stop Carmen from leaving. "Let me go or kill me," she demanded[1].

Then, she took off[2] the gold ring that Don Jose had given her and threw[3] it at him. "Don't ever give me anything ever again," she snapped.

At that moment, Don Jose took out[4] his knife and pushed it into[5] her heart. She fell into his arms, and he wept[6] into her hair. His heart was truly[7] broken[8].

Perhaps another man may have tried to escape but he did not. He stayed there with her so the police could find him.

"My life is over. My life finished when she stopped loving me and now I have killed the most precious[9] thing in the world. My life is worthless[10] so it doesn't matter[11] what happens to me," he wept.

---

1. **demand** [dɪˋmænd] (v.) 要求
2. **take off** 脫下
3. **throw** [θrəʊ] (v.) 扔；拋
4. **take out** 拿出
5. **push into** 推入
6. **weep** [wiːp] (v.) 流淚；悲泣
   (weep-wept-wept)
7. **truly** [ˋtruːli] (adv.) 真正地
8. **broken** [ˋbroʊkən] (a.)
   破碎的
9. **precious** [ˋprɛʃəs] (a.) 珍貴的
10. **worthless** [ˋwɜːrθləs] (a.)
    無價值的

The police came and took him to prison. Carmen was given the most beautiful funeral[12]. She is dead but her love for life and freedom[13] will always be alive[14]. Fate came to take her away. She accepted[15] her fate just like we all should.

11. **matter** [ˋmætə(r)] (v.)
　　要緊；重要
12. **funeral** [ˋfjuːnərəl] (n.) 喪禮
13. **freedom** [ˋfriːdəm] (n.) 自由

14. **alive** [əˋlaɪv] (a.)
　　存在的；活潑的
15. **accept** [əkˋsept] (v.) 接受

A Choose the correct answer.

1 The _____ tell you about your future destiny.

(a) teachers　　(b) fortune-tellers

(c) bullfighters　(d) smugglers

2 When Carmen went to see the bullfight, there were many other _____.

(a) spectators　(b) gypsies

(c) soldiers　　(d) fighters

B Fill in the blanks with the given words.

kill	want	reply	return	look

Just then, Carmen and the smugglers **1**_____ to the camp. One of the smugglers said to Escamillo, "He **2**_____ you unless you leave right now." The bullfighter **3**_____, "Alright. I will go. But I **4**_____ to invite you all to the bullring on Sunday to see me fight." Escamillo **5**_____ directly at Carmen and said, "And those who love me are especially welcome to come and see me."

Aida

阿伊達

Before You Read

Princess Amneris

My name is princess Amneris. I live in the most beautiful palace in Egypt. I have everything I want except my true love, Radames. I dream of marrying him some day, but there is one who stands in my way.

Aida

My name is Aida. I am a slave, but once was a princess. I am in love with an Egyptian general. It is hard for me as my country, Ethiopia is at war with Egypt. But I know he loves me and it is our destiny to be together.

Radames

My name is Radames. I am the General of the Egyptian army. I will soon go to war against Ethiopia. If I am victorious, I will be able to marry my sweetheart. I would do anything to be with her.

Amonasro

I'm Amonasro. I am the King of Ethiopia. My country is at war with Egypt. I do miss my daughter, Aida. She was taken from me by the Egyptian army. I pray she is still alive, she is such a beautiful girl. When will I see her again?

Chapter One

🎧27 Amneris vs. Aida

I am Princess Amneris. My father is the King of Egypt. I live in a wonderful place. It is the most beautiful palace, and I can have anything I want.

I never have to work because there are servants[1] to do everything for me. I wear the most beautiful clothes everyday. They are made by hand from the best silk in the world. I wear diamonds, rubies[2], emeralds[3], gold and silver.

1. **servant** [ˈsɜːrvənt] (n.) 僕人
2. **ruby** [ˈruːbi] (n.) 紅寶石
3. **emerald** [ˈemərəld] (n.) 綠寶石
4. **general** [ˈdʒenərəl] (n.) 將軍
5. **miserable** [ˈmɪzrəbəl] (a.) 難受的；悲哀的
6. **cry oneself to sleep** 哭著睡著
7. **comfort** [ˈkʌmfərt] (n.) 安慰

I have the best of everything. But it is not enough. It will never be enough unless I can have Radames. I am so in love with Radames. He is the general[4] of my father's army, and he is such a handsome and powerful man.

I am so miserable[5]. No one knows how miserable I am. Every night, I cry myself to sleep[6] because Radames does not love me the way I love him. No one can give me any comfort[7] except for him.

🎧 28

Yesterday was a terrible[1] day. We are at war with[2] the Ethiopians[3], and Ramfis, the High Priest[4], said to Radames, "The King wants you to take our army to Ethiopia to fight our enemies[5]."

Everyone in the palace thinks it is such a high honor[6]. I guess it really is, but I worry so much about him. I cannot help but[7] imagine his body lying[8] dead[9] on the ground somewhere. Men never know how women worry about them so much.

But then I also had an idea. If Radames is victorious[10], then my father will order him to marry me. That would be wonderful.

1. **terrible** [ˈterəbəl] (a.) 可怕的
2. **be at war with** 與⋯⋯戰爭
3. **Ethiopian** 衣索匹亞人
4. **priest** [priːst] (n.) 祭司；神職人員
5. **enemy** [ˈenəmi] (n.) 敵人
6. **honor** [ˈɑːnər] (n.) 榮譽；榮耀
7. **cannot help but** 不得不
8. **lie** [laɪ] (v.) 躺；臥
9. **dead** [ded] (a.) 死的；喪生的

Some time ago, I thought he would come to love me. We used to[11] spend a lot of time together. We used to walk together beside[12] the River Nile in the evening. My servants would always stay[13] further[14] behind. They knew that I wanted to be alone[15] with him. No doubt they gossiped[16] a lot about Radames and myself.

It has always been hard to hide my feelings but now I am better at it. Even my closest[17] friend doesn't know how I feel about Aida.

10. **victorious** [vɪk`tɔɪriəs] (a.) 勝利的

11. **used to** 過去一向……

12. **beside** [bɪ`saɪd] (prep.) 在旁邊

13. **stay** [steɪ] (v.) 逗留；留在

14. **further** [`fɜːðər] (a.) 較遠的

15. **alone** [ə`loʊn] (a.) 單獨的；獨自的

16. **gossip** [`gɑːsɪp] (v.) 說閒話

17. **closest** 最親近的 （close 的最高級）

Aida! She is an Ethiopian woman. She was caught[1] in battle[2] and my father gave her to me as a slave[3].

She really is an amazing[4] woman. She speaks so well and when she walks, she is so elegant[5]. It almost seems that she is a noble[6] woman instead of[7] a slave.

In the palace, she learned to do everything so quickly, and she never seems to be bitter[8]. In the beginning, it was very easy to be friendly[9] and kind to her. I often forgot that she was born an enemy of my country.

1. **catch** [kætʃ] (v.) 抓住
   (catch-caught-caught)
2. **battle** [ˋbætl] (n.) 戰鬥;戰役
3. **slave** [sleɪv] (n.) 奴隸
4. **amazing** [əˋmeɪzɪŋ] (a.)
   驚人的
5. **elegant** [ˋelɪgənt] (a.) 優美的
6. **noble** [ˋnoubəl] (a.)
   高貴的;貴族的
7. **instead of** 代替

8. **bitter** [ˋbɪtər] (a.) 不滿的
9. **friendly** [ˋfrendli] (a.) 友好的
10. **detest** [dɪˋtest] (v.) 厭惡
11. **gaze at** 凝視;注視
12. **catch one's breath** 屏息
13. **jealousy** [dʒeləsi] (n.) 嫉妒
14. **ceremony** [ˋserəmouni] (n.)
    儀式;典禮
15. **shake** [θeɪk] (v.) 發抖;搖
16. **pale** [peɪl] (a.) 蒼白的

There is one problem. She is beautiful.
It wouldn't matter if I was more beautiful than
her, but Radames seems interested in her.
I detest[10] that.

When they are in the same room together,
they act differently. Radames gazes at[11] her
repeatedly. She catches her breath[12] when he
speaks. Every time I see this, I am filled with
jealousy[13].
   Why does Radames want her more than me?
She is only a slave but I am a princess!

Yesterday, in the ceremony[14] when Radames
became the General of the Army, Aida was
there. She was shaking[15]. I know what she was
thinking. She doesn't want to think of him
dying in battle.
   At the end of the ceremony, everyone cried
out, "Victory to Egypt!" At that moment, she
turned pale[16] and later I heard her crying. I was
the only one who knew why.

My name is Aida. I became a slave in the Egyptian palace after I was caught in a battle. No one really knows who I am. I am an Ethiopian princess.

When I first came here, it was a horrible[1] time for me. Everyone treated[2] me terribly. Every night, I used to cry from homesickness[3].

Now I keep[4] my pain[5] deep inside and do not let anyone see it. And I have to be careful that no one finds out that I'm a princess.

Sometimes I wonder[6] how I can continue[7] with my life in this palace. But there is one thing that even though[8] it gives me pain, it also gives me happiness. I am in love with Radames. So I have two secrets[9] that I must keep. Both are very hard to keep.

1. **horrible** [ˋhɑːrəbəl] (a.) 恐怖的；駭人的
2. **treat** [triːt] (v.) 對待
3. **homesickness** [ˋhoumsɪknəs] (n.) 鄉愁
4. **keep** [kiːp] (v.) 使保持……
5. **pain** [peɪn] (n.) 痛苦
6. **wonder** [ˋwʌndə(r)] (v.) 懷疑
7. **continue** [kənˋtɪnjuː] (v.) 繼續
8. **even though** 即使；雖然
9. **keep a secret** 保守秘密

I sometimes wonder how I can love an Egyptian. He is the enemy of my country. In fact, he is probably[1] the greatest enemy. It is his job to plan battles against my country.

This tears me apart. I feel that if I love him, I am betraying[2] my country and people. But also, if I am loyal[3] to my country, then I am lying to the man I love.

1. **probably** [ˋprɑːbəbli] (adv.) 或許
2. **betray** [bɪˋtreɪ] (v.) 背叛；不忠
3. **loyal** [ˋlɔɪəl] (a.) 忠誠的；忠心的
4. **shout out** 大叫出來
5. **allow to** 允許……
6. **for joy** 欣喜地
7. **defeat** [dɪˋfiːt] (n.) 失敗；戰敗

Yesterday, Radames became the General of the Army. It was all I could do to stop myself from running from the ceremony.

It was very hard for me to see. Of course I had to shout out[4], "Victory to Egypt."

Later, Ramades came to me and said, "I can ask to marry you if I return victorious. The King will have to allow me to[5] marry you."

When I heard him say that, my heart jumped for joy[6]. But I cannot wish for him to return victorious if it means the defeat[7] of my people.

Princess Amneris is another problem.
At first¹, she was very kind to me. But that
slowly changed as time went on².

I know, as well as³ many of the other slaves
and servants, that she loves Radames. I have
heard her laughing and talking about him with
other servants and slaves. But
she never does this in front
of me. Has she
discovered that
Radames and I love
each other?

She almost never
speaks to me now. Did
she see us together?
I need to be more careful.

1. **at first** 起先
2. **go on**（時間）過去
3. **as well as** 也；和
4. **suspicion** [səˋspɪʃən] (n.)
   懷疑
5. **matter** [ˋmætə(r)] (v.)
   有關係；要緊
6. **find out** 發現

"Amneris! You are being foolish." I have thought about this so many times. My suspicions[4] are making my life miserable. I cannot live like this, worrying about Radames and Aida.

The battle is over and Radames is coming home. But Aida does not know this yet.

I spoke to my father and he agreed to tell Radames that he must marry me. So it won't matter[5] anymore if Aida loves Radames.

Still, I must find out[6] if Aida loves Radames. If I don't, I will never be able to sleep at night.

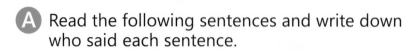

A Read the following sentences and write down who said each sentence.

Amneris

Aida

1 I am princess of Egypt. I live in a wonderful place.

_____

2 I became a slave in the Egyptian palace after I was caught in a battle. _____

3 I sometimes wonder how I can love an Egyptian.

_____

4 I spoke to my father and he agreed to tell Radames that he would marry me. _____

5 I have the best of everything. _____

B Rewrite the sentences with "used to."

> We walked together beside the River Nile.
> ⇨ We *used to* walk together beside the River Nile.

1 I thought that one day he would love me.

⇨ _____

2 It was easy to be kind and friendly to Aida.

⇨ _____

C True or False.

1. Radames loved Amneris a long time ago.   T   F
2. Radames has been the priest of the Country   T   F
   for a long time.
3. Every servant knew that Amneris loved   T   F
   Radames.
4. Aida was an ordinary woman in her country.   T   F
5. It is difficult for Aida to love Radames.   T   F

D Fill in the blanks with the given words.

comfort myself army miserable honor enemies

No one knows how **1**_____ I am. Every night, I
cry **2**_____ to sleep because Radames does not
love me the way I love him. No one can give me any
3_____ except for him. Yesterday was a terrible
day. Because we are at war with the Ethiopians, Ramfis,
the High Priest, said to Radames, "The King wants
you to take our **4**_____ to Ethiopia to fight our
5_____." Everyone in the palace thinks it is such a
high **6**_____.

Slaves
in Ancient Egypt

It was common in ancient times for warring nations to take slaves from enemy countries. This is what happened to Aida, the Ethiopian princess.

Although she is a slave and Ethiopian, she falls in love with an Egyptian general. When a war breaks out again between Ethiopia and Egypt, she is torn between her country and her new love.

Slaves in ancient Egypt were of many kinds. Some people were born into slavery, some were bought and sold like cattle, and some were won in war.

While slaves did die from overwork in the desert mines or in large buildings like the pyramids, many royal slaves were treated quite well. They were actually better off than many free Egyptian peasants.

Aida is a slave to royalty, so she is treated well. However, many other slaves were beaten, or did not receive enough food and water to live well. Life was very hard for slaves in ancient times.

· Chapter Two ·

🎧33 The Deception[1]

Amneris has played such a trick[2] on me. She is a cruel[3] woman. She did it just before the victory parade[4]. It was a very hot and terrible day for me. I had to stand by[5] and watch my people being dragged[6] through the streets. All of the Egyptians were cheering[7] and shouting out, "Victory to Egypt!"

Horses came by[8] and they were pulling carts[9] full of gold and precious things from my country.

Amneris was standing in front of me. She was dressed beautifully. Her clothing[10] was sparkling[11] from the emeralds and rubies and gold sewn[12] through it.

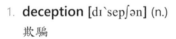

1. **deception** [dɪˋsepʃən] (n.) 欺騙
2. **play a trick** 施詭計
3. **cruel** [kruːəl] (a.) 殘酷的
4. **parade** [pəˋreɪd] (n.) 遊行
5. **stand by** 站在旁邊
6. **drag** [dræg] (v.) 拖；拉
   (drag-dragged-dragged)

7. **cheer** [tʃɪr] (v.)
   歡呼；喝采

8. **come by** 從旁邊走過去

9. **cart** [kɑ:rt] (n.) 雙輪載貨車

10. **clothing** [ˋkloʊðɪŋ] (n.)
    衣服；衣著

11. **sparkle** [ˋspɑ:rkəl] (v.)
    閃耀；發光

12. **sew** [soʊ] (v.) 縫
    (sew-sewed-sewn)

She tricked[1] me while we were still in her room. She said to me in a sad voice, "This would be a happy day if Radames had not been killed in battle."

Her words shocked[2] me and I burst into tears[3]. I covered my face and cried and cried.

Then Amneris said to me in a cruel voice, "Stop it, Aida. Radames is not dead. You love him, don't you? I suspected[4] you did and now I have found out."

1. **trick** [trɪk] (v.) 欺騙
2. **shock** [ʃɑːk] (v.) 震驚；衝擊
3. **burst into tears** 突然哭起來
4. **suspect** [sə`spekt] (v.) 懷疑
5. **hiss** [hɪs] (v.) 發噓聲表示輕蔑；斥責
6. **dry** [draɪ] (v.) 把……弄乾
7. **suitable** [`suːtəbəl] (a.) 適合的

Again, I was shocked. I should have suspected her lie. I was so foolish not to.

She hissed[5] at me, "You are nothing more than a slave. My father has promised that Radames will marry me. Stop crying and dry[6] your eyes. You must come with me to the victory parade. You must see Radames promising to be MY husband."

I felt such pain. If only I could tell her that I was a princess, too. If only she knew that I was suitable[7] to be the wife of a noble man, too.

I was nearly[1] crying, thinking of this at the parade when something even more terrible happened. I saw my father, Amonasro among my country's people being dragged in the streets.

I ran to his side[2]. "Father! Father! What have they done to you?"

I cried out. But my father hushed[3] me. "Shh! Don't say anything. They cannot find out that I am the King of Ethiopia. If they do, they will kill us both. We must be quiet," he said.

The Opera Stories: Aida

I went to the King of Egypt to beg[4] for my father's life. "Your Majesty[5]! This man is my father. Since you have been so kind to me, please set these people free[6]. They are not criminals[7]," I begged.

But then, Ramfis said, "We should kill them all. Kill all of the Ethiopians!"

Radames looked shocked and quickly said, "No, we won the battle. We have their gold and their land. Let's not take their lives[8]. Let them go."

1. **nearly** [ˋnɪrli] (adv.)
   近乎；幾近
2. **side** [saɪd] (n.) 旁邊；身邊
3. **hush** [hʌʃ] (v.)
   使安靜；噤聲
4. **beg** [bɛg] (v.) 乞求

5. **Your Majesty**
   陛下（第二人稱之稱呼）
6. **set free** 釋放
7. **criminal** [ˋkrɪmɪnəl] (n.) 罪犯
8. **take one's life**
   奪走某人的生命

Ramfis then said, "Alright, let them go. But keep Aida and her father. They must stay hostages[1] in Egypt."

The King agreed to this. The King now looked at Radames and embraced[2] him like a son. I knew what would happen next. I felt my heart hit the ground.

"Radames! You are the greatest warrior[3]. You are the victor in this war, so you should receive the greatest prize[4] of all. I give you Amneris to be your bride[5]."

1. **hostage** [`hɑːstɪdʒ] (n.) 人質
2. **embrace** [ɪm`breɪs] (v.) 擁抱
3. **warrior** [`wɔːriə(r)] (n.) 戰士；勇士
4. **prize** [praɪz] (n.) 獎賞；獎品
5. **bride** [braɪd] (n.) 新娘

I heard the words and even though I knew they were coming, I could not know how badly I would feel. I could not breathe[6] and I felt my soul[7] had been taken from me.

I looked at Radames. He had turned pale[8]. He looked at me and in his eyes I could see his love for me. My own eyes were filling with tears. What would we do?

6. **breathe** [briːð] (v.) 呼吸
7. **soul** [soʊl] (n.) 靈魂；心靈
8. **turn pale** 變蒼白

I arranged to[1] meet Radames on the bank[2] of the River Nile. It is so beautiful there in the evening. The evening was very clear, and I could see each star twinkling[3] in the sky. It was like they knew the pain deep in my heart.

I meant to[4] put an end to[5] my miserable life, and the reason I wanted to meet Radames was to say goodbye to him.

I went to the river and waited. I heard a noise in the reeds[6] by the river and I said, "Radames?" But he didn't reply.

It was my father. "I have to speak to you," he said.

"Speak quickly father," I replied.

I didn't want Radames to see me with my father. I wanted our final meeting to be perfect, just between the two of us.

1. **arrange to** 準備；安排
2. **bank** [bæŋk] (n.) 河岸
3. **twinkle** [ˋtwɪŋkəl] (v.) 閃耀
4. **mean to** 意圖；打算
   (mean-meant-meant)
5. **put an end to** 結束
6. **reed** [riːd] (n.) 蘆葦
7. **attack** [əˋtæk] (v.) 進攻

My father quickly spoke, "One day you will be princess again. The Egyptians are planning to attack[7] our soldiers, and we must be ready for them this time. We must find out where they are going and wait for them so that we can surprise[8] them with an attack."

My father looked lovingly[9] into my eyes. He knew how sad I was and how I longed to[10] return to my country.

"But what can I do?" I asked my father.

He replied, "You must try to find out from Radames which way his army will go."

"But how can I ask him to betray his own country?" I asked, feeling very confused[11].

"You must," ordered[12] my father. "If you don't, then you will be betraying your own country. I will hide in the reeds and listen to everything."

My father left me and hid among the reeds to wait for Radames.

8. **surprise** [sə`praɪz] (v.)
出其不意
9. **lovingly** [`lʌvɪŋli] (adv.)
慈愛地
10. **long to** 渴望
11. **confused** [kən`fjuːzd] (a.)
困惑的
12. **order** [ɔːrdə(r)] (v.) 命令

Radames finally came. "My love, I have missed[1] you so much. Please don't marry Amneris. Let's leave this place so that we can be together," I said to him. But I knew in my heart that I couldn't ask him to run away[2] with me.

Surprisingly[3] he said, "Yes, let's go away together. We can take the same road that the army will take on its way to Ethiopia. We will go along[4] the Napata Gorge[5]."

Just as he said that, my father came out of[6] the reeds and said, "Radames, I am the King of Ethiopia."

1. **miss** [mɪs] (v.) 想念
2. **run away** 逃跑
3. **surprisingly** [sə`praɪzɪŋli] (adv.) 驚人地
4. **go along** 沿著……走
5. **gorge** [gɔːrdʒ] (n.) 峽谷
6. **come out of** 從……走出來

The Opera Stories: Aida

Then there was some noise in the reeds. Apparently[7] someone else had been listening to our conversation, too.

Amneris! She called the priests from the temple and ordered them to arrest Radames. She looked extremely[8] angry.

"You have betrayed me and your country, Radames! I am so disappointed in[9] you," she said.

Radames now said, "I must accept my punishment[10] and go with the priests. Aida, run away! Go with Amonasro. Go now before it is too late!"

My father took me away and we ran into the darkness of the night.

7. **apparently** [ə`pærəntli]
(adv.) 顯然地
8. **extremely** [ɪk`striːmli]
(adv.) 極其地；非常地
9. **be disappointed in**
對……失望
10. **punishment** [`pʌnɪʃmənt]
(n.) 處罰；刑罰

What is the use of[1] being the Princess when
I cannot sleep for the sorrow[2]?

Radames came to see me in my room
tonight. I said to him, "Try to love me and
I will go to my father and beg for mercy[3].
He will spare[4] your life for me."

All he said was, "That is very kind of you Princess Amneris, but I have no reason to live. Aida is gone and I don't want to live without her. I heard she and her father were captured[5] and killed."

I quickly replied, "No. Her father was captured, but she managed to[6] escape. If you give up[7] your love for her, I will save[8] you. I love you just as much as she does."

His next words broke my heart. "I could never love you, Amneris. I will go and wait for my death," he said.

He walked out of the room and out of my life. I never saw him again. He was placed[9] in a prison under the temple[10]. He will die a very sad death in that cold, lonely place.

1. **What is the use of . . . ?**
   ……有什麼用？
2. **sorrow** [ˋsɑːrou] (n.) 悲哀
3. **mercy** [ˋmɜːrsi] (n.)
   仁慈；寬容
4. **spare** [sper] (v.)
   赦免；饒恕
5. **capture** [ˋkæptʃə(r)] (v.)
   俘虜
6. **manage to** 設法做到
7. **give up** 放棄
8. **save** [seɪv] (v.) 拯救；救出
9. **place** [pleɪs] (v.) 放置
10. **temple** [ˋtempəl] (n.) 神殿

I have finally found a place where I can be happy. I returned to the temple by[1] the River Nile. I knew that the priests would lock[2] Radames in the prison under the temple, so I went there to wait for him.

"Radames, my love! I came to be with you and to die with you. Let us die together and escape this world of pain[3]. Let's go to a better place together," I said to him. We lay[4] in each other's arms, finally happy together.

1. **by** [baɪ] (prep.)
   靠近；在……旁邊
2. **lock** [lɑːk] (v.) 鎖；鎖住
3. **pain** [peɪn] (n.) 痛苦

4. **lie** [laɪ] (v.) 躺臥；斜倚
5. **imprison** [ɪmˋprɪzən] (v.)
   監禁
6. **by now** 此刻

It has been a long time since the priests imprisoned Radames. He must be dead by now.

I never found out what happened to Aida. Perhaps my jealousy killed them both. I found out later that she too was a princess. We could have been such good friends. Instead, I was unkind to her.

I cry every night for Radames. If Aida is dead, then I cry for her too. I hope they can both find happiness in their next lives.

A Select the synonym of the underlined words.

1 The King now looked at Radames and <u>embraced</u> him like a son.

(a) hit   (b) advised

(c) looked   (d) hugged

2 He knew how I <u>longed</u> to return to my country.

(a) wanted   (b) hated

(c) succeeded (d) was able

3 You are the victor in this war, so you should receive the greatest <u>prize</u> of all.

(a) money   (b) reward

(c) salary   (d) punishment

B Fill in the blanks with proper names from opera *Aida*.

1 _____ played a terrible trick on Aida.

2 The King announced that _____ would marry Amneris.

3 _____ met Radames on the bank of the River Nile.

4 _____ saw Radames talking to _____ and ordered the priests to arrest them.

Appendixes

1. Basic Grammar
2. Guide to Listening Comprehension
3. Listening Guide
4. Listening Comprehension

1

Basic Grammar

要增強英文閱讀理解能力，應練習找出英文的主結構。
要擁有良好的英語閱讀能力，首先要理解英文的段落結構。

「英文的閱讀理解從「分解文章」開始」

　　英文的文章是以「有意義的詞組」（指帶有意義的語句）
所構成的。用（／）符號來區別各個意義語塊，請試著掌握其
中的意義。

He knew　／　that she told a lie　／　at the party.

他知道　　她說了謊　　　　　　　　在舞會上

⇨ 他知道她在舞會上說謊的事。

As she was walking　／　in the garden,　／　she smelled　／

當她行走　　　　　　　在庭院　　　　她聞到味道

something wet.

某樣東西濕濕的

⇨ 她走在庭院時聞到潮溼的味道。

一篇文章，要分成幾個有意義的詞組？

可放入（／）符號來區隔有意義詞組的地方，一般是在（1）「主詞＋動詞」之後；（2）and 和 but 等連接詞之前；（3）that、who 等關係代名詞之前；（4）副詞子句的前後，會用（／）符號來區隔。初學者可能在一篇文章中畫很多（／）符號，但隨著閱讀實力的提升，（／）會減少。時間一久，在不太複雜的文章中即使不畫（／）符號，也能一眼就理解整句的意義。

使用（／）符號來閱讀理解英語篇章
1. 能熟悉英文的句型和構造。
2. 可加速閱讀速度。

該方法對於需要邊聽理解的英文聽力也有很好的效果。
從現在開始，早日丟棄過去理解文章的習慣吧！

以直接閱讀理解的方式，重新閱讀《杜蘭朵公主》

　　從原文中摘錄一小段。以具有意義的詞組將文章做斷句區分，重新閱讀並做理解練習。

My life / has been full of adventure.
我的生活 / 一直以來充滿冒險

Now that I am very old, / telling stories / is all I can do.
現在我已經很老　　　 / 說故事　　　 / 是我唯一可做的

My name / is Calaf.
我的名字 / 是卡拉富

I was born / the Prince of Tartary.
我生下來 / 是韃靼的王子

After a very long and terrible war, / my father, King Timur, and I / were forced to escape / from my country.
在一場漫長殘暴的戰爭中　　　　　/ 我的父親，帖木兒國王和我 /
被迫逃離　　　　/ 從我的國家

I didn't know / what happened / to my father / but now I was in Peking.
我不知道　　/ 發生什麼事　　/ 對我父親　　/ 但現在我在北京

I would never forget / the evening / I arrived in this great city.
我絕不會忘記　　/ 那一晚　　/ 我抵達這個雄偉的城市

Many people had gathered / in the square / in front of the Imperial Palace.
許多人群聚集　　　　　/ 在廣場　　　/ 在紫禁城前面

It was really amazing.
那真的很壯觀

There must have been / thousands of people / there.
一定有　　　　　/ 好幾千人　　　　/ 在那兒

I thought / that something very exciting / was to occur, / so I asked, / "What's happening?"
我想　　/ 刺激的事情　　　　/ 就要發生　　　/ 所以我問
/ 發生了什麼事

One person in the crowd / replied, / "A man will be killed soon.
人群中有一個人　　　/ 回答　　/ 有一個人馬上要被處死

He had come / to try to marry / Princess Turandot.
他來到這兒　/ 想要娶　　/ 杜蘭朵公主

He had to solve / the Princess's riddles first / before he could marry her, / but he failed.
他必須解答　　/ 公主的謎語　　　　　/ 在他娶她之前
　　/ 但他失敗了

Now / they will cut off his head."
現在 / 他們要砍下他的頭

"Who is Princess Turandot?" / I asked.
杜蘭朵公主是誰　　　　　　　/ 我問

"She is the Emperor's daughter," / said a woman / standing next to me.
她是皇帝的女兒　　　　　　　　/ 一個女人說　　/ 站在我旁邊

"She is extremely beautiful.
她非常美麗

So / many princes come / from different countries / to marry her.
因此 / 很多王子前來　　/　　來自不同國家　　/ 要娶她

But / she doesn't want to marry / any of them.
但是 /　　她不想嫁給　　/ 他們當中任何一個

She is a cold woman.
她是冷漠的女人

Some say / that her heart is made from stone.
有人說　　/ 她的心是石頭做的

To make it difficult / for any man to marry her, / she has said / that she will only marry the man / who can solve the three riddles / she gives them.
要使其變得困難　　/ 任何男人娶她　　　　　　/ 她說過
/ 她只會嫁給　　　　　　/ 能解開三個謎語的男人
/ 她對他們提出的

If they fail, / well,... you can see / what we are waiting for . . ."
如果他們失敗 / 那麼……你就可以看到 / 我們面前在等的下場了

Guide to Listening Comprehension

 When listening to the story, use some of the techniques shown below. If you take time to study some phonetic characteristics of English, listening will be easier.

Get in the flow of English.

English creates a rhythm formed by combinations of strong and weak stress intonations. Each word has its particular stress that combines with other words to form the overall pattern of stress or rhythm in a particular sentence.

When speaking and listening to English, it is essential to get in the flow of the rhythm of English. It takes a lot of practice to get used to such a rhythm. So, you need to start by identifying the stressed syllable in a word.

Listen for the strongly stressed words and phrases.

In English, key words and phrases that are essential to the meaning of a sentence are stressed louder. Therefore, pay attention to the words stressed with a higher pitch. When listening to an English recording for the first time, what matters most is to listen for a general understanding of what you hear. Do not try to hear every single word. Most of the unstressed words are articles or auxiliary verbs, which don't play an important role in the general context. At this level, you can ignore them.

Pay attention to liaisons.

In reading English, words are written with a space between them. There isn't such an obvious guide when it comes to listening to English. In oral English, there are many cases when the sounds of words are linked with adjacent words.

For instance, let's think about the phrase "**take off**," which can be used in "take off your clothes." "Take off your clothes" doesn't sound like [teɪk ɔːf] with each of the words completely and clearly separated from the others. Instead, it sounds as if almost all the words in context are slurred together, [ˈteɪkɔːf], for a more natural sound.

Shadow the voice of the native speaker.

Finally, you need to mimic the voice of the native speaker. Once you are sure you know how to pronounce all the words in a sentence, try to repeat them like an echo. Listen to the book again, but this time you should try a fun exercise while listening to the English.

This exercise is called "shadowing." The word "shadow" means a dark shade that is formed on a surface. When used as a verb, the word refers to the action of following someone or something like a shadow. In this exercise, pretend you are a parrot and try to shadow the voice of the native speaker.

Try to mimic the reader's voice by speaking at the same speed, with the same strong and weak stresses on words, and pausing or stopping at the same points.

Experts have already proven this technique to be effective. If you practice this shadowing exercise, your English speaking and listening skills will improve by leaps and bounds. While shadowing the native speaker, don't forget to pay attention to the meaning of each phrase and sentence.

Step 1 Listen to what you want to shadow many times. Start out by just trying to shadow a few words or a sentence.

 Step 2 Mimic the CD out loud. You can shadow everything the speaker says as if you are singing a round, or you also can speak simultaneously with the recorded voice of the native speaker.

 Step 3 As you practice more, try to shadow more. For instance, shadow a whole sentence or paragraph instead of just a few words.

Listening Guide

以下為《歌劇故事》各章節的前半部。一開始若能聽清楚發音，之後就沒有聽力的負擔。先聽過摘錄的章節，之後再反覆聆聽括弧內單字的發音，並仔細閱讀各種發音的説明。以下都是以英語的典型發音為基礎，所做的簡易説明，即使這裡未提到的發音，也可以配合音檔反覆聆聽，如此一來聽力必能更上層樓。

Chapter One page 16 🎧41

My life has been full of adventure. Now that I am very old, telling stories is all I can do. My name is Calaf. I was born the Prince of Tartary.

After a very long and terrible war, my father, King Timur, and I (❶) ( ) ( ) escape from my country. I didn't know what happened to my father but now I (❷) ( ) ( ).

I would never forget the evening I arrived in this great city. Many people had gathered in the square (❸) ( ) ( ) the Imperial Palace. It was really amazing. There (❹) ( ) ( ) thousands of people there. I thought that something very exciting was to occur, so I asked, "What's happening?" One person in the crowd replied, "A man will be killed soon.

❶ **were forced to:** 在此動詞詞組中，forced 的發音聽起來最強，應熟記 forced 的 -ed 和 to 連著一起發音，在一篇文章中，基本上意義較不重要的助動詞、介系詞、代名詞等，聽起來會比較弱。

❷ **was in Peking:** was 和 in 連著發音，當 in 快速唸過並發音微弱，常會聽起來像 [n] 的音，而 Peking 是專有名詞。即使是聽簡短的文句，若有專有名詞在其中，因不熟悉發音，有時會感到慌張。因此當出現外來語或專有名詞時，應逐漸養成注意重音和發音的習慣。

❸ **in front of:** in front of 是常使用的介系詞片語，應熟記 front 和 of 是發連音，-nt 的 [t] 發音會不明顯，與 -nt 相連的單字，[t] 音消失是美語的特徵，另一個例子是 internet 的發音。

❹ **must have been:**（過去一定是……），這類的助動詞片語，通常是快速地發弱音略過，幾乎聽不到各個單字的發音。與 must 連在一起發音，have 的 [h] 音消失變成連音，通常以 h 開頭的助動詞（have、has 等）或代名詞（him、her 等）發弱音時，[h] 音會略過聽不見。

(❶) ( ) ( ) ( ). I do not need to tell you my name. It is not important (❷) ( ) ( ). The only name you really need to remember is the name Carmen. In a small town, there was a man named Jose. He (❸) ( ) soldier and he lived in the army barracks, which were on one side of the town square. On the other side, there was a cigarette factory.

One day, a girl named Micaela went to this town. She came from the country and Jose was her sweetheart. (❹) ( ) ( ) she arrived at the square, she spoke to the Captain of the Guard.

❶ **I am from Spain:** Spain 的 p 發音是不送氣的 [p] 音，s 後若緊接著 [p]、[t]、[k] 等音，就會變成不送氣音，這是英語發音的特徵。至 於 Rome、Paris 的英語發音，和我們母語的發音方式完全不同的情形很 多。請務必熟記常出現的地名。

❷ **for this story:** this story 的 this 和 story 相連，兩個 s 只發音一次，當 相同的音連在一起，不會各自單獨發音，summer 的 [m] 音就是一個例 子。

❸ **was a:** was 和 a 連在一起發音，這兩個單字常相連出現，這類的發音聽 起來像一個單字，應熟記。

❹ **As soon as:** 這也是常出現的片語，應熟悉發音和語調。

I am Princess Amneris. My father is the King of Egypt. I live in a wonderful place. It is the (❶) ( ) ( ), and I can have anything I want. I never have to work (❷) ( ) ( ) servants to do everything for me. I wear the most beautiful clothes everyday. They are made by hand from the (❸) ( ) in the world. I wear diamonds, rubies, emeralds, gold and silver. I have the best of everything.

❶ **most beautiful palace:** most beautiful 中 -st 和 b 相連時，[t] 音有時會被省略，而三個子音相連，其中的音常會被省略，英文是偏向簡單發音的，並記住 beautiful 和 palace 重音是第一音節。

❷ **because there are:** 這裡最容易聽清楚的音是 -cause，因為 because 的重音在第二音節，相對地第一音節的發音聽起來較弱，有時甚至只聽到第二音節的發音。there are 不具有重要的意義，所以常發輕音並快速帶過。

❸ **best silk:** best silk 中 -st 和 s 相連，[t] 音會被省略，前後兩個 s 會只發一個音，最後的 [k] 音在口語中應該像幾乎聽不見，才最接近英語的標準音。

4

Listening Comprehension

🎧 44 **A** Listen to the CD, write down what you heard and select the correct person who is described in each sentence.

ⓐ Turandot   ⓑ Carmen   ⓒ Aida   ⓓ Amneris

1 _____ _____

2 _____ _____

3 _____ _____

4 _____ _____

🎧 45 **B** Listen to the CD and fill in the blanks.

1 My life has been full of _____.

2 Right at that moment, I did something which would _____ _____ _____ forever.

3 Red was for a _____ and white was for a _____.

4 Once more, he begged me to go but I wanted to answer the _____.

5 I was so stunned by Liu's _____ to my father and myself.

🎧 46 **C** Listen to the CD, write down the question and choose the correct answer.

❶ _____?

   (a) He thought he was innocent.

   (b) He was so scared that he couldn't move at all.

   (c) He felt his life was worthless and he didn't care about the future.

❷ _____?

   (a) Because she was tired of him and she started to love another man.

   (b) Because she was so worried about Jose's sick mother.

   (c) Because she felt sorry for Micaela.

🎧 47 **D** Write down what you heard, and circle either True or False.

T F **❶** ....

T F **❷** ....

T F **❸** ....

T F **❹** ....

T F **❺** ....

《杜蘭朵公主》（Turandot）

《杜蘭朵公主》出自以《托斯卡》（Tosca）和《蝴蝶夫人》（Madam Butterfly）出名的義大利作曲家普契尼（Puccini），也是其最後也最偉大的作品。

場景設定在古代中國北京，講述冷血的杜蘭朵公主設計三道謎語並處死無法解謎的求愛者，而韃靼國的卡拉富王子是如何融化了公主的心，幫助她瞭解真愛的意義。

1920 年，普契尼深受故事背景裡中國古代的異國與神話情調吸引，決定將 18 世紀義大利作家卡洛‧戈齊（Carlo Guzzi）撰寫的故事改編成歌劇。然而，在完成這齣三幕的歌劇前，普契尼即去世，之後由他的朋友兼同事弗蘭科‧阿爾法諾（Franco Alfano）完成終幕。

1926 年 4 月 25 日，《杜蘭朵公主》在斯卡拉歌劇院歷史性首演，由托斯卡尼尼擔任指揮。首演的第三幕，在普契尼筆下，劇情來到柳兒死亡之時，托斯卡尼尼放下指揮棒，面朝觀眾說：「歌劇未完但已結束，因為大師在此時去世。」此景也成了一段著名的軼事。

卡門（Carmen）

1875 年，法國最偉大的作曲家比才（Bizet, 1838–1875）根據法國劇作家梅里美（Merimee）的故事完成歌劇《卡門》。唐荷西是個天真的年輕准將，駐守於西班牙塞維亞，有未婚妻與病中母親在家鄉等候。某天，因為迷戀上菸廠工作的吉普賽女人卡門，他拋棄了遠大的職業前程與未婚妻。然而他很快地發現，卡門已將情感轉移到鬥牛士艾斯卡密羅身上，在絕望的憤怒中，唐荷西在廣場刺死卡門。

《卡門》於 1875 年在巴黎首映時飽受嚴苛批評，因過於傷風敗俗與粗俗，未能吸引巴黎貴族。然而在比才去世後，作品重新搬上舞台並贏得滿堂彩。自始，《卡門》成為舉世著名的歌劇之一。

阿伊達（Aida）

《阿伊達》是創作《弄臣》（*Rigoletto*）與《茶花女》（*La traviata*）的義大利作曲家朱塞佩‧威爾第（Giuseppe Verdi）的傑作之一。此劇是受埃及政府之託，為了開羅歌劇院的開幕而作，而歌劇院的建造則是為慶祝 1869 年秋天蘇伊士運河（Suez Canal）的啟航日。

1871 年，《阿伊達》在開羅新歌劇院的啟用儀式首演。雖然《阿伊達》是為慶祝而生之劇，卻描寫一段悲傷的愛情故事。

年輕的埃及將軍拉達梅斯愛上埃及公主安納瑞斯的奴隸、原為衣索比亞公主的阿伊達。然而，阿伊達在對拉達梅斯的愛與對故土的情中拉扯，而她與拉達梅斯的社會地位不同，也使她遭受苦痛。

同時，也喜歡拉達梅斯的安納瑞斯公主得知兩人的愛情，心生嫉妒，決心阻擾兩人，最終這對命運多舛的戀人一同離開了人世。

《阿伊達》場景設定於古代埃及，被認為是偉大的歌劇之一。劇中描寫祖先崇拜儀式與舞蹈的場景，為《阿伊達》增添華麗與異國情調。

朱塞佩‧威爾第將普世的人類情感，如愛憎、希望與死亡，予以強調並穿越時空，揉合成富麗壯觀、如若人生的劇情。這齣劇巧妙地將精緻而多元的戲劇元素編織成壯麗的故事，因而飽受好評。

p. 14–15 ## 人物簡介

Calaf 卡拉富

我叫卡拉富，是韃靼國的太子。我已經垂垂老矣，但年輕時也曾經驚濤駭浪過。當時我痛失一位摯友，還改變了一個很特別的人的一生。你喜歡猜謎嗎？我很喜歡。

Princess Turandot 杜蘭朵公主

我是杜蘭朵公主。很多男人來向我求婚，但我不想嫁給他們。光宗耀祖才是要緊事，不是嗎？想娶我的人，要是不夠聰明，就得付出代價！

King Timur 帖木兒大帝

我是帖木兒大帝。一場戰爭讓我亡國，後來我又在逃亡期間雙目失明。我一直在尋找太子卡拉富，我們在戰亂中失散了。幸好多虧有婢女柳兒在身邊帶著我，要是沒有她，我真不知道該怎麼辦。

Liu 柳兒

我叫柳兒，是帖木兒大帝的婢女。戰後，我便一直服侍著大帝。侍候大帝和皇室家族是的我職責。我很仰慕卡拉富，唯願早日與他重逢。

[第一章] 冷若冰霜的公主

p. 16–17 我的一生歷經過各種風浪，如今我老了，只有陳年往事可以說。我叫卡拉富，是韃靼的太子。

在一場漫長而艱鉅的戰爭之後，我和帖木兒父王被迫流亡異國。我這時來到了北京，但父王下落不明。

進京後的這一晚，我畢生難忘。當時，宮殿前的廣場上圍聚了成千上萬的人民，場面驚人。

　　我心想，必定是要發生什麼大事，便問路人：「怎麼回事？」

　　有一個人回答說：「有人要被處決了！那個人原本是想來娶杜蘭朵公主的，但是他沒有答對公主出的謎題，所以現在要被斬首了！」

p. 18–19 「誰是杜蘭朵公主？」我問。

　　「她是皇帝的女兒。」站在我身邊的一名婦人說：「她美若天仙，很多國家的太子都跑來想娶她，但她誰也不想嫁。她冷若冰霜，鐵石心腸。

　　想娶她呀，難如登天！她出了三道謎題，規定只有能解謎的人才能娶她，如果答不出來，那就……你等一下就可以看到下場了……」

　　此時，走出一名穿著官服的人，他喊道：「波斯王子未能解答公主的謎題，今晚月亮東升之時，即行處決。」

　　當我聽著這則公告時，後面傳來了聲響。我回過頭，看見一位老翁跌倒在地上，一名婦人大喊：「看啊！他們竟然將可憐的失明老人推倒在地。」

　　我趕過去，扶老翁站起來，卻嚇了一大跳！那名老翁竟就是父王帖木兒大帝。「父王！」我大叫：「您來北京了，我一直到處在找您啊。」

p. 20–21 我抬頭，看見站在一旁的人，正是柳兒。她為人忠心，對父王來說，她亦僕亦友。「柳兒！妳也在這兒！」

　　父王說：「多虧了她！自從我失明了以後，她就有如我的雙目，幫了我很多的忙。要不是因為有她，我這條命早就沒了！」

柳兒低著頭，看著自己的腳。

我問她：「柳兒，妳這樣照顧父王，我感激不盡！妳本不需這樣做的，為什麼妳願意為我們一家人付出這麼多？」

她回答：「以前在宮殿裡，你老是對我眉開眼笑……」她的話此刻被一陣響亮的鑼聲給打斷。

有一批人湧進廣場，搬來一塊大石頭，安置在廣場中央。那塊石頭是要給劊子手磨斧頭要用的。

「月亮一升起來，就砍下他的頭！」眾人喊著。

我聽了很震驚，他們似乎很期待看到人被斬首！

我心想：「這些人與禽獸何異，而杜蘭朵公主又怎麼忍心處決那麼多人？她果然是一個冷血的人。」

`p. 22-23` 眾人繼續呼叫，要求處決那名可憐人。但當公主一出現時，頓時鴉雀無聲。

公主一身白袍，遠望就像冰做的一般；她髮如黑緞，幾乎長及地面；她貌美無瑕，朱唇豔如玫瑰。

她啟唇下令道：「來人！把他押下去斬了！」

那位可憐的王子隨即被拖出去處決。那是個駭人的夜晚，我卻無暇念及那個可憐人！

我像是中了邪一般，滿腦子裡只有公主。我直楞楞地盯住公主，傾心不已，一時之間幾乎停止了心跳！

`p. 24-25` 接下來，我做了一件足以改變我一生的決定。我大聲地喊道：「我來此，是為了向公主求婚的！我會解開她的謎題，娶她為妻。」

柳兒聽了叫道：「不！不！你會被斬首的，一想到這，我就無法忍受！」

父王也懇求我說：「我會再次痛失愛子的，請不要啊。」但我置若罔聞，逕自走向廣場中央的大鑼。凡是要向公主求親的人，都要敲鑼三次。

我走近大鑼，有三個人前來阻攔我。

其中一人說：「我是宰相，平。」另一個人說：「我是御廚，彭。」第三個人說：「我是將軍，龐。」

「別敲鑼啊！」他們三人同聲高呼。

龐說：「你看天上！難道你沒看見死者的魂魄盤旋京城不散嗎？他們都是求親不成的幽魂啊。」

平說：「世間上美女如雲，去找其他的女子吧！」

我只道了一個「不」字，便從他們中間走過，直往大鑼敲了三次。

p. 26–27 眾人目睹我敲鑼，我聽到了他們的唏噓聲：「他猜不出謎底的。」

三位大臣也互相說道：「今年已經有十三個人斷送命了，京城內腥風血雨啊。」

眾人莫不認為我必死無疑，但我決志不改，一心想娶公主。沒多久，來了兩名差役，帶我進宮。

半晌後，一群大學士拿著一大批卷宗走出來，我猜卷宗裡頭就寫了公主的謎題。

隨後，又走進來幾個人，手上各拿著紅燈籠與白燈籠，分別代表著婚慶與喪禮。

最後，走出來的是皇帝，一臉愁容。

他看著我，說道：「別猜謎了，別猜我女兒的謎題了。趁她還沒出來前，你走吧！」

我回答：「我不走，我要猜謎。」皇帝又勸了我兩次，但我執意一試。

p. 30-31 **紫禁城**

在歌劇《杜蘭朵公主》中所描繪的紫禁城，已不同於今日。這齣歌劇由義大利歌劇作曲家普契尼所作，但普契尼未曾去過中國，其靈感實是來自馬可波羅的遊記。

一千年前左右，馬可波羅到中國遊歷，紀錄下位於首都北京城中央一座小丘上、城牆高聳的神秘紫禁城。之所以稱作紫禁城，是因為只有皇室貴族與其僕役才得以進入。劇中，杜蘭朵公主是在紫禁城城門對群眾說話的。

在馬可波羅的時代，北京的街道寬敞筆直。馬可波羅形容其街道猶如棋盤，建築整齊，古色古香的樓宅和豪華客棧林立。

今日紫禁城的圍牆與建築依舊，但城門已為來自世界各地的遊客敞開。杜蘭朵和中國的帝王之家已不復存在，但他們曾經居住過的京城仍歷久不衰。

[第二章] 三道謎題

p. 32 又過了半晌，杜蘭朵公主走了出來。她立如白燭，至美至雅。她開口說話，我心跳得簡直要进出胸口。

她說：「我要為先祖樓林公主報一箭之仇。一千年前，一名異族王為了樓林公主進攻此城，並奪色謀害了她。為了彰明她的貞烈，我誓言不近男子。現在你要回答三道謎題，只要答錯一題，你命便休矣。」

我答道：「謎題有三道，人生只有一回。」

p. 34-35 她開始問我第一道謎題：「什麼魔，住於人心，一入夜就生，太陽一升起又滅？」
我細細思索後，回答：「希望。」

在我說出答案後，她顯得不安。她繼續問我第二道謎題：「什麼東西，暖如火，熱時滾燙，死時冷卻，勝利時耀如夕照、熾情沸沸？」

我又仔細思量，答道：「血。」

杜蘭朵滿心不悅地瞪著我，眼神冷酷如冰。她接問最後一道謎題：

「什麼冰，能灼燒人，然既能吞噬人，卻又讓人更備感冰凍？」

廣場上眾人靜待動靜，這次我推敲良久。

「杜蘭朵！」最後我終於回答：「杜蘭朵，妳冷若冰霜，但我對你情熱如焚。就是你，燒耗了我的思緒情感！」

p. 36–37 立在雄偉宮殿廣場上的大學士們，詫然地搖著頭。我已經解開三道謎題了！有好一會兒，杜蘭朵一臉震驚。

接著，她急忙在皇帝跟前下跪，懇求道：「請不要將我許配給他，求求您，父王！」

但皇上回答：「他三道謎都已經解開，我們承諾過，只要誰能解開，就能娶到公主，不可違諾！」

這時，杜蘭朵站起來，轉身看我，問道：「難道你想結一場非兩廂情願的親事？」

我回答：「不想，我當然不想！所以，只要妳能夠在天亮前猜出我的名字，我非但不會逼婚，也甘於受妳處決！」

這番話讓杜蘭朵聽了很安心，她又露出她那種不懷好意的淡淡一笑，說道：「很好，我今晚不查出你的名字，誰都別想上床睡覺！你就等著明天人頭落地吧！我將重金懸賞，查出你的名字！」

當晚，京城內無一人能安睡。我在宮庭的花園裡靜待太陽升起，平、彭、龐三位大臣前來探視我，又勸我說：「公主必定能查出你的名字的，在公主處決你前，你就悄悄地離開吧。」

這時，庭院內傳來的一陣嚷嚷聲。我急奔過去，看到了幾個差役拖著我父王和柳兒來到庭院裡。

其中一名差役說：「這兩個人昨天和他說過話，知道他是誰。」

我急忙喊道：「不，他們不知道我是誰！我是在昨天才認識他們的！」

p. 38–39 等杜蘭朵一來，差役便開始毆打我父王。柳兒喊道：「請不要打他啊，他只是一位老人家，你們想知道的事情，只有我才能告訴你們。」

我想前去阻止柳兒開口，但被差役給攔住。

杜蘭朵命令道：「把她帶下去，打到她肯說為止。」

柳兒叫道：「我不會說的，寧死不說！」

柳兒對父王和我的忠誠讓我震驚不已，連杜蘭朵都不禁問她：「妳何苦那麼在意他？何苦為他犧牲性命也在所不惜？」

柳兒回答：「因有情故，所以無畏。妳心若冰石，但終將被他的情意所融。」

她說罷便往前一躍，抓住一名差役的匕首，直往自己的胸口刺下去。一切發生得太突然，沒人來得及阻止。柳兒就這樣在我面前倒下，香消玉殞。

p. 40 可憐的柳兒，為我捨命，令我痛心疾首！

我轉過身，對杜蘭朵說：「妳這個死神之女，妳所到之處，死亡如影隨形！」

杜蘭朵看著我，說道：「錯了，我是天帝之女，魂神同天遨翔，非你們這些凡夫俗子所能及！」

「妳的魂神或許在天，但妳與我同處塵世，與他人無異！」我說完，便走到她面前，扯下她的面紗，摟住她奪吻。她起初如野獸般拚命抗拒，但我溫情的親吻融化了她冰冷的心，令她淚湧而下。

我對她說：「我充滿情意的親吻，溫暖了妳的芳心，妳再也不是冷若冰霜的公主了。」

p. 42–43 「我第一眼見到你，我就知道你會帶給我痛苦。你走吧！我不想知道你的名字了，不用說你的名字了。」她說。

我回道：「我既然勝了，也不在乎生死了。我叫卡拉富，韃靼國的太子。」

稍晚，旭日東昇。皇帝上朝，我和杜蘭朵站在朝廷上。皇帝先對杜蘭朵說：「杜蘭朵，妳查到他的名字了嗎？」

「查到了，父王。他叫做『有情』。」她回答。接著，她露出前所未見的微笑，笑中不再挾著怨恨，而是充滿情意。

平、彭、龐贊許地直點頭，皇帝也一副龍心大悅的樣子。後來，我和杜蘭朵成親，生活幸福，共度年歲。能和所愛之人白頭偕老，實一大樂事。

卡門

p. 46–47 **人物簡介**

Carmen 卡門

我叫卡門，吉普賽人。我熱愛生命，熱愛自由。男人動不動就敗倒在我的石榴裙下，真是一群傻子！他們不是想要我，就能得到我的，而我呢，倒是一向想要誰，就能要誰。我相信命運，你呢？

Don Jose 唐荷西

我叫唐荷西，是一名軍人。做軍人的最大福利，就是中午的換班時間，我喜歡趁那時候在廣場上尋找工廠美麗女工的倩影。我老巴望著能有一親芳澤的機會。

Micaela 蜜凱拉

我是蜜凱拉，從鄉下來的，是唐荷西的女友。唐荷西是個好人，但我常常抓到他在看別的女人，這讓我很不安。

Escamillo 艾斯卡密羅

我叫艾斯卡密羅，是一名鬥牛士，大都在星期天於群眾面前表演鬥牛。很多女子喜歡看我鬥牛，因為我穿上鬥牛士服裝後魅力十足。

[第一章] 吉普賽女郎與軍人

p. 48–49 我來自西班牙，但我不需報上名來，因為這無關緊要。你唯一需要記住的名字是「卡門」。在一個小鎮上，有個叫唐荷西的軍人，住在軍隊營房。軍營就位在市中心廣場旁，廣場的另一邊則是一間製菸工廠。

一天，一位名叫蜜凱拉的姑娘來到鎮上。她是從鄉下來的，唐荷西是她的心上人。

她一抵達廣場，便對衛兵長說：「抱歉，我要找唐荷西，我是從他的家鄉來的，帶了一封他母親的信要給他。」

衛兵長回答：「衛兵中午會換班，他那時候就會來了，妳可以在這兒等他。」

「謝謝你。」她說。

p. 50–51 在一旁等候的蜜凱拉，這時聽到了一聲哨音響起，那是製菸工廠工人午餐時間的哨音。工廠女工傾巢而出，來到廣場吃午餐，而卡門也身在其中。

卡門，是出乎筆墨所能形容的。她是吉普賽女郎，她的魅力讓每個男人都為之傾倒。

她美豔動人，熱情如火，只可惜容易生膩。她可以很快愛上一個男人，也可以一下子就拋之棄之。

她熱愛自由，只想當選擇的一方，而非被選擇。她自由如鳥，寧為自由亡，也不願被關在籠中。

她老對朋友說：「沒有男人可以選擇我，只有我才能決定要愛誰。」

p. 52–53 女工的午餐時間，正逢衛兵換班。

一行士兵走踏步走進廣場，他們一見到卡門，就沒了個樣子，全跑過來和她打情罵俏，想得到她的青睞，但她只是對著他們的傻樣子笑了笑。

「你們何必這樣花心思呢？難以到手的男人，我才有興趣呀！愛情啊，不是那樣簡單的一回事。當人不期待時，愛情才會到來。」

當時唐荷西也在廣場上，他對卡門一見傾心，直盯著她不放。卡門驀地一回首，也看到了唐荷西。

就在這時，工廠的哨音又響起，卡門對友人喊道：「弗拉斯基塔！麥賽德絲！我們得回去工作了。」

然而，卡門並未直接走回工廠，反而走向唐荷西。她取下她美麗秀髮上的一朵紅玫瑰，扔到唐荷西的腳邊，對他嫣然笑著。

p. 54–55 在故事發生的那個時代，很多人都相信命運，相信凡事都受命運所主宰。

唐荷西心裡明白，只要他撿起那朵玫瑰，他就會永遠成為她的俘虜，如此一來，卡門將可以對他予取予求。

他們互相凝視著，一陣靜默之後，唐荷西彎下腰，撿起了玫瑰。現在，他已經屬於卡門的了。他神魂顛倒，他未來的福分，只能聽任命運了。

等工廠女工都離開後，蜜凱拉走進廣場。唐荷西一見到她，又驚又喜，也很高興收到母親的信。只不過，蜜凱拉或家書都無法攫住他的注意力，他的心神早已飄到別處了。

唐荷西不想和蜜凱拉多談，蜜凱拉怏怏然地離開。蜜凱拉一離開後，唐荷西便幾乎忘了她的存在。

p. 56–57 一天，工廠裡發生爭執，卡門打傷了另一名女工。事情發生的緣由無人知曉，總之，卡門遭到逮捕。軍中長官祖尼卡命令唐荷西率領一組士兵，將她送進監獄。

　　卡門一見到唐荷西，又是嫣然一笑。

　　「是命運撮合了我們！待會我們過橋的時候，你放我走，之後我會在里拉酒館等你。我保證我將只愛你一個人！」

　　唐荷西回答：「這不行啊，我得送妳去監獄。」

　　「你一定要放了我，你的心早已受我主宰了！你撿起玫瑰的時候，那朵神奇的玫瑰就把我們緊緊綁在一起了。難道你感覺不出來嗎？」她說道。

　　唐荷西陷入天人交戰。卡門說得沒錯，他必須放了她。最後在她逃走之際，她說：「里拉酒館！別忘了！」

p. 58–59 祖尼卡得知卡門逃走後，氣憤不已。

　　「你這個大白癡！你讓她給跑了，你就自己去吃牢飯吧。把他關進監獄裡！」

　　其實大家都知道，祖尼卡也很愛慕卡門。事實上呢，把情敵送進監獄，他倒是鬆了一口氣。可憐的唐荷西，一心期待只想盡早見到卡門。

　　幾個月後的一個夜晚，卡門與朋友弗拉斯基塔、麥賽德絲，一道現身里拉酒館。她們喝著酒，和幾個走私販聊著天。

　　祖尼卡也在酒館裡，他多次乞求卡門把唐荷西忘掉。「唐荷西想必是已經把妳忘掉了！」

　　祖尼卡對卡門說：「妳以為他會來這裡找妳，只可惜他不會啊。他今天出獄，可是也沒見他來！」

　　卡門回答：「他愛我，他會來的。我也答應過要等他，我得信守諾言。」

p. 60–61 就在這時，弗拉斯基塔說道：「聽啊！是艾斯卡密羅的行進隊伍啊，他們要前往賽維爾，我們快去看吧！」

　　艾斯卡密羅是一名鬥牛士，總是穿著一套合身的緞質衣服，非常體面，很多女子都覺得他非常英俊瀟灑。

他走進酒館，看到了卡門，便問道：「妳叫什麼名字？」

她回答：「我是卡門。」

「等一下鬥牛時，我要用妳的名字來當護身符。」這時每個人都看得出來，卡門用充滿熱情的眼神看著艾斯卡密羅。

艾斯卡密羅來到酒館，是命運的安排。如果他那天晚上是去了別的地方，那這個故事的結局就會完全不同。

p. 62–63 艾斯卡密羅離開後，唐荷西走進酒館大門。卡門跑向他，他開口說道：「卡門吾愛！妳真的在這裡，遵守了妳的諾言。」之後，他們共舞到天明。

唐荷西：「我得走了，天亮了，我得回軍營了。」她懇求著：「不要回去，留下來，我們去加入走私販那一幫人吧！我們可以住在山上，享受自由。」

他回答：「我不能擅離職守。」卡門聽了，一步步往後退，說道：「我沒法愛一個懦夫的，你要是不肯為我冒險，那就表示你不愛我。」

她似乎要找個理由讓唐荷西可以離開她，她才可以投向艾斯卡密羅的懷抱。

她又說：「跟我們一起來吧！」

唐荷西答道：「我愛妳，我跟你們一起走！」

唐荷西於是和卡門一起加入了山上的走私販。

p. 66–67 吉普賽人的生活

卡門是吉普賽人，所以她的生活看似浪漫不羈。當代的科學研究顯示，吉普賽人是在一千年前離開印度後，開始了流浪生活的一個民族，十六世紀時來到歐洲。

很多歐洲人、甚至連吉普賽人本身，都認為吉普賽人的祖先來自埃及。而這也就是「吉普賽」一詞的由來，他們先是被稱為 Egyptians（埃及人），接著變音為 Gyptians，最後演化成 Gypsies。

　　吉普賽人抵達歐洲時，歐洲大部分的地方都已經有人定居，況且他們又不像多數歐洲人一樣信仰基督教；再加上他們的膚色較深，語言文化都不同，等等原因造成歐洲人並不歡迎吉普賽人。因此吉普賽人居無定所，並多有吉普賽人好行巫術、性格浪蕩的傳聞。

　　卡門代表了吉普賽人這種浪蕩不羈的形象。她的西班牙士兵情人，因為無法駕馭她，轉而殺了她。不幸的是，這樣的情節在歐洲歷史上不斷上演，吉普賽人因天生的與眾不同，而遭受磨難。

[第二章] 艱困悲慘的生活

`p. 68-69` 唐荷西和卡門的生活一片慘澹，毫無安逸之處可言。夏天，露宿星空下；冬天，就睡在又舊又髒的帳棚裡。

　　一開始，彼此還有熱情可撐下來，但沒多久卡門就膩了。

　　有一天，卡門說道：「你該回家去的，這種生活不適合你，回到你母親身邊，回到家鄉吧！你唯一適合做的，就是穿著你那楞頭楞腦的軍服，四處去行軍。」

　　「我是想離開，但我不會那麼做。我愛妳，所以我要和妳一起待在這裡，我絕對不會離開妳的。」他回答。

`p. 70-71` 「但是這裡的生活這麼苦，你以後會因此懷恨我，說不定你哪一天會殺了我。」卡門說道。

　　卡門老會想到死亡。不久前，她和朋友在玩紙牌算命時，弗拉斯基塔說：「我要愛情！我要一個會永遠愛我的年輕男人。」

　　麥賽德絲笑著說：「我要老男人，我要一個活不久的有錢老頭，把他的財產全都留給我！」

就在大家說著彼此的命運時，卡門抽出了一張紙牌，她們把那張牌放回去洗牌。

她再抽了一次，卻抽中同樣的一張牌。

她的朋友喊道：「黑桃二，妳抽了兩次都是黑桃二。」

黑桃二，只代表了一種意義：死亡。卡門說：「所以我活不久了，紙牌是很準的。」她知道死亡正等著她，無可改變。

p. 72–73 第二天，蜜凱拉來到走私販的營地，她是來找唐荷西的。這時她撞見另一人也來到了營地，便迅速躲到一塊大石頭後面。

來人正是鬥牛士艾斯卡密羅。唐荷西一見到他，就拿起槍準備對著他射擊。

艾斯卡密羅喊道：「我不是警察，別射我，我只是來找卡門的！」

唐荷西問道：「她要是不願意跟你一起走呢？」

艾斯卡密羅回答：「我知道她會跟我走的！我們第一次見面時，她看我的眼神就別有不同。和軍隊的逃兵混在一起，是沒什麼好處，她會跟我走的！」

唐荷西警告他道：「要從男人那裡搶走吉普賽女人，可是很危險的。」

艾斯卡密羅笑一笑，說道：「話是沒錯，不過你不是吉普賽人，況且你還是個軍人。」

p. 74–75 就在此時，卡門和走私販返回營地。其中一名走私販對艾斯卡密羅說：「你快走吧，他會殺了你的。」

鬥牛士回答：「好吧！我走！不過我要邀請你們所有人星期天來鬥牛場看我鬥牛。」

艾斯卡密羅眼睛直視著卡門說道：「特別是那些欣賞我的人，更是歡迎之至！」艾斯卡密羅說罷，便離開了營地。

147

他一離開，躲在一旁蜜凱拉走了出來，說道：「唐荷西的母親有口信要給他，他母親病了，想見他一面。

「唐荷西，和我一起走吧！」

卡門對唐荷西說：「的確，你是應該回去。」唐荷西轉向她，問道：「然後呢？離開妳讓妳去向艾斯卡密羅投懷送抱？」

卡門坦言不諱答道：「沒錯！我對你已經沒有感情了！我們之間結束了！」

唐荷西於是打包準備離開營地。離開前，他顫抖著聲音對卡門說：「我保證我們還會再見面的！」

p. 76–77 下一件大事是發生在幾星期後。一個星期日，賽維爾要舉辦一場重要的鬥牛賽，鬥牛場上擠滿了觀眾。

艾斯卡密羅抵達鬥牛場，卡門隨行在旁，貌似比從前更加明豔動人。

而這卻徒讓在觀眾群中等待她的唐荷西，更加妒火中燒。

弗拉斯基塔和麥賽德絲看到唐荷西，便勸道：「卡門！他在這裡啊！妳一定要小心呀！」

「不，我會走去看他，如他所願。我不會逃跑的。」

卡門跑去找唐荷西，對他說：「我朋友說你也在這兒，她們擔心你會殺了我！」

他回答：「我並不想殺妳，我只是希望妳能繼續愛我！沒有了妳，生命一無是處！求妳回到我身邊吧！」

「記著，我要愛誰，是由我來選擇的！我已經不愛你了！我得走了，鬥牛結束了。」她說。

唐荷西惱羞成怒，喊道：「妳愛的是他吧？妳別否認了！」

她笑著說道：「我才沒否認呢！我就是愛他！」

p. 78–79 他不讓卡門離開，卡門命令地說：「放了我！不然就殺了我！」

148

說罷，她便拔下唐荷西送的金戒指，往他面前扔去，氣憤地說道：「以後別再送我任何東西了！」

就在此刻，唐荷西亮出他的刀子，往她的心臟刺了進去。她倒在他懷裡，他的眼淚沾濕了她的頭髮，心碎不已。

換成別的男人，可能會趕緊逃逸，但他沒有。他守在她身邊，直到警察發現了他。

「我的生命結束了！從她不再愛我那一刻起，我的生命就結束了！我毀了世上最珍貴的東西，我的命一文不值了！再也沒有什麼事是要緊的了！」他悲泣道。

之後警察過來將他帶到監獄。

卡門的喪禮甚為莊嚴，她已離世，但她對生命與自由的熱愛，卻永存不滅。命運帶走了她，她接受了命運，而人們也應該如是而行。

阿伊達

 **p. 82-83 人物簡介**

Princess Amneris 安納瑞斯公主

我是安納瑞斯公主，住在埃及最華麗的宮殿裡。我擁有一切，卻得不到我的真愛拉達梅斯。我一直夢想有天能嫁給拉達梅斯，但卻有人礙事。

Aida 阿伊達

我叫阿伊達，是奴隸也曾是公主。我愛上了一位埃及將領，卻愛得很苦，因為我的祖國衣索匹亞正和埃及在交戰。然而我知道他也愛我，而我們也注定會在一起。

Radames 拉達梅斯

我是拉達梅斯，是率領埃及軍隊的將軍。我很快就要去征戰衣索匹亞，只要我得勝，就能和心愛的人結婚。為了能與她在一起，我不惜一切代價。

Amonasro 阿摩納斯洛

我是阿摩納司洛，衣索匹亞的皇帝，我國正和埃及開戰中。我很想念我女兒阿伊達，埃及軍隊把她從我身邊奪走，我祈禱她還活著。她是這麼可愛的一個女孩，我要何時才能再見到她啊？

[第一章] 安納瑞斯與阿伊達

p. 84–85 我是安納瑞斯公主，我的父王是埃及國王。我住在一個再好不過的地方了，這裡有最華麗的宮殿，我要什麼就有什麼。

我什麼都不用做，僕人會幫我打理一切；我每天穿的都是錦衣繡服，綾羅綢緞，我穿金戴銀，一身鑽石寶石。

什麼至寶至珍的東西，我都擁有。但是光有這些東西並不夠，除非我得到了拉達梅斯，不然我永遠不滿足。我深愛著拉達梅斯，他是我父王軍隊的將軍。他美若潘安，又擁有權勢。

我過得很痛苦，沒有人能了解箇中滋味。我夜夜淚濕枕頭，因為拉達梅斯並不愛我，一如我愛他那樣。除了他，無人能夠安撫我的痛苦。

p. 86–87 昨天是個可怕的日子！我們和衣索匹亞開戰，我們的大祭司朗費司對拉達梅斯說：「國王命令你率軍，前去征戰敵國衣索匹亞！」

皇宮裡每個人都認為這是無上光榮，這的確是沒錯，但我實在很擔心拉達梅斯！我老想到他橫屍沙場的畫面，我克制不住呀！男人永遠都不了解女人如何為他們憂心如焚。

然而，我也有另一種想法：如果拉達梅斯打了勝仗，父王就會命令他娶我，如果真是那樣，就太好了！

不久前，我還以為他會愛我。過去，我們時常在一起。夜晚我們會沿著尼羅河一起散步，僕人們會遠跟在後，他們知道我想和他獨處。顯然他們會對我和拉達梅斯的事竊竊私語。

要我隱藏自己的感受，實在很困難。但現在，我可以隱藏得好一些，即使是我最親密的朋友，也不知道我對阿伊達的想法。

p. 88–89 阿伊達是個衣索匹亞女子，她在戰爭中被俘虜，父王把她送給我做奴僕。但她很不可思議，講話得體，舉止又很優雅，看起來反倒像是貴族，而非奴隸。

在宮裡，她什麼事都學得很快，也未見她有過愁容。她很容易讓人有一見如故的感覺，我常會忘了她是敵國的人呢。

但有一個問題：她長得花容月貌。我要是長得比她美，那就不成問題，但問題是，拉達梅斯似乎對她頗有好感。我痛恨這一點！

他們只要同在一室，行為就會失常。拉達梅斯常不時盯著她瞧，而她在聽拉達梅斯說話時，總會屏氣凝神。只要我一看到這種場面，我就妒火中燒。

為什麼拉達梅斯要的是她，而不是我？她不過是個奴婢，我才是公主呀！

昨天，在拉達梅斯授命為將軍的儀式上，阿伊達也在場。她渾身顫抖，我知道她心想什麼，她不希望他戰死沙場！典禮最後，眾人齊喊：「埃及勝利！」這時阿伊達臉色一陣蒼白，接著我聽到了她啜泣的聲音，而我是唯一知道原因的人。

p. 90–91 我叫阿伊達，在戰爭中被敵人俘虜，成了埃及的宮奴。沒有人知道我真實身分，而我其實是衣索匹亞的公主。

剛到埃及時是最可怕難熬的，我飽受人人欺凌，每晚都因思鄉而哭泣。

但現在我把痛苦深藏起來，不讓人知道。我務必小心，以免讓人發現我的公主身分。

有時我很懷疑自己怎能在這個皇宮裡活下去。然而，還有一件事，只要一想到這事我就深感痛苦，卻又深感快樂：我愛上了拉達梅斯。現在，我有這兩個秘密得守著，但無論是哪一個秘密，都很難守住。

p. 92–93 有時我會納悶自己怎會愛上一個埃及人，他是我國的敵人，事實上還可算上是最大的敵人，他的任務是和我國作戰。

這讓我有著撕裂般的痛苦。我感到若我愛著他，就等於背叛了我國和人民；同樣地，若我忠於自己的國家，那我就是欺騙了我愛的人。

昨天，拉達梅斯成了統領全軍的將軍，而我唯一能做的，就是忍住不從典禮上逃走。看著典禮進行，我萬分痛苦，況且我還得跟著大喊：「埃及勝利！」

典禮過後不久，拉達梅斯走到我面前對我說：「等我凱旋歸來，就可以要求娶妳為妻，那時國王是必得應允我的。」

當我聽到他這麼說時，我的心雀躍不已。然而，如果這表示我的國家會被打敗，那我就不能期望他凱旋歸來呀！

p. 94–95 安納瑞斯公主是另一個問題。一開始，她對我很和善，可是卻漸漸有了改變。

和其他很多奴僕一樣，我知道她也很愛慕拉達梅斯。我聽過她和奴僕們有說有笑地在聊拉達梅斯，但她卻從不這樣跟我聊。難道她已經看出來我和拉達梅斯彼此屬意？

現在她幾乎不和我講話了，她是不是看過我們在一起？我得更加小心才行。

〔安納瑞斯獨白〕我好幾次罵自己說：「安納瑞斯！妳這個大笨蛋！」我疑神疑鬼，日子過得很痛苦啊。

我不能再這樣下去，不能再這樣把心懸在拉達梅斯和阿伊達兩人身上。戰爭已結束，拉達梅斯即將歸國，但阿伊達還不知道這事。

我已向父王開口，父王也答應命令拉達梅斯娶我為妻，所以阿伊達是否愛著拉達梅斯，就再也不重要了！

不過，我還是得弄清楚她到底愛不愛拉達梅斯，不然我夜裡就永遠無法睡得安穩。

p. 98–99 古埃及的奴隸

在古代，戰俘常會被帶回戰勝國當奴隸，這也是衣索匹亞公主阿伊達的遭遇。

儘管她變成了奴隸，又是衣索匹亞人，但她和一位埃及將軍互相意屬。當兩國再度爆發戰爭時，祖國和心上人的衝突令她痛苦萬分。

古埃及的奴隸分成很多種，有些是奴隸階級出身的，有些是像牲畜般買賣而來的，有些則是戰俘。有些奴隸會因會過勞，而魂斷沙漠礦坑或大型建物如金字塔，但皇宮內的奴隸，卻往往生活無慮，事實上，他們的生活過得比很多自由的埃及農民還好。

阿伊達就是一名宮奴，因此受到不錯的對待。然而，有很多奴隸仍是過著常遭毒打、食物匱乏的生活。古代奴隸的生活，是很艱辛困苦的。

[第二章] 欺騙

p. 100 就在慶祝勝利的大遊行之前，安納瑞斯對我施了個詭計，她的心真狠。那天，天氣炎熱，對我來說尤其悲慘。我得站在路旁，一路目睹我的人民在大街上被拖著前進。街上埃及人民歡騰不已，齊聲歡呼：「埃及勝利！」

成群的馬匹拉著一輛輛馬車經過，車上滿載從衣索匹亞奪來的黃金和寶物。

　　安納瑞斯當時就站在我的前面，她一身華服，衣服上綴滿寶石和黃金，金光閃閃。

p. 102-103 之前我們在她房間時，她對我撒了謊。她故作傷心地騙我說：「如果拉達梅斯沒有戰死沙場，那今天就可喜可賀了！」

　　她的話讓我震驚不已，我的眼淚奪眶而出，掩面哭泣。

　　安納瑞斯狠心地對我說：「別哭了，阿伊達！拉達梅斯並沒有死。妳愛他，對吧？我以前就懷疑妳了，果不其然呀！」

　　她的這番話，又讓我震驚。我應該早猜得出來她是在撒謊，我真是太不機靈了！

　　她對我叱喝道：「妳只是個奴隸！父王已經答應要讓拉達梅斯娶我了，妳不准再哭了，把眼淚擦乾！現在，妳要陪我去參加慶祝勝利的遊行，妳得看著拉達梅斯親口承諾要娶我！」

　　我感到萬分痛苦，我真想告訴她我也是公主，也是可以和貴族成親的！

p. 104-105 遊行時，一想到這些，我忍不住就要哭了出來，但此時，更可怕的事情發生了！在戰俘遊行隊伍中，我看見了父王阿摩納斯洛！

　　我跑向他，哭喊道：「父王！父王！他們對你做了什麼呀？」

　　父王要我別出聲：「噓！不要說話，不要讓他們知道我是衣索匹亞國王，不然我們倆都會沒命的！不要作聲！」

　　我走到埃及國王面前，乞求他饒我父王一命。我懇求道：「國王陛下！這人是我父親，您對我一向很仁慈，我請求您放了這些人！他們不是罪犯啊！」

但祭司朗費司說道：「我們應該把他們全都殺了！殺光衣索匹亞人！」

拉達梅斯面露震驚，立刻說道：「不可以，我們贏了戰爭，佔有了敵國的黃金和土地，別再奪走他們的性命，放了他們吧！」

p. 106–107 朗費司說：「好吧！放了他們！不過把阿伊達和她父親留下，留在埃及作為人質。」

埃及國王表示同意。接著，國王看了看拉達梅斯，像父親擁抱兒子般地擁抱了他。我知道接下來會發生什麼事，我一顆心猛然下沈。

「拉達梅斯！你是最偉大的戰士，你打贏了這場戰爭，應該得到最大的賞賜！我要把安納瑞斯賜給你，招你為駙馬！」

我真的聽到這番話了！雖然我早就知道了，卻沒料到親耳聽到這些話會讓我如此難受。我無法呼吸，失了魂一般。

我看著拉達梅斯，他臉色刷白。他望向我，眼神裡充滿愛意。我淚眼婆娑，我們該怎麼辦呀？

p. 108–109 我約了拉達梅斯到尼羅河邊相會。河邊夜色如水，星光點點，彷彿看穿了我內心深沈的痛苦似的。

我打算結束我痛苦的生命，所以我想再見拉達梅斯一面和他告別。

我走到河邊，等著他來。這時河邊蘆葦叢中傳出聲響，我問道：「是拉達梅斯嗎？但聲音沒有回應。」原來那是我父王。他說：「我有話要跟妳說。」

「請快說，父王。」我回答。

我不想讓拉達梅斯瞧見我和父王在一起。我希望我和他的最後一面能兩人獨處，盡善盡美。

我父王很快地說道：「妳總有一天會再做回公主的！埃及

155

人正計畫攻打我軍，這次我們會做好萬全準備來迎戰。我們要查出他們的路線，一路埋伏，再加以突擊！」

父王慈愛地看著我，他知道我過得很苦，很想回到自己的國家。

我說：「但我能做什麼？」

他回答：「從拉達梅斯的身上問出軍隊出征的路線！」

我茫然無緒，問道：「我怎能要求他背叛自己的國家？」

父王命令道：「非得這麼做不可，不然妳就是背叛自己的國家了。我會躲在蘆葦叢，細聽你們的談話。」

說罷，父王便躲進蘆葦叢，等待拉達梅斯的到來。

p. 110–111 最後，拉達梅斯終於來了。我對他說：「吾愛，我好想你啊，請不要和安納瑞斯成親，我們離開這裡，這樣我們就可以在一起了！」但我內心明白，我不能強求他和我一起遠走高飛。

未料，他竟回答：「好，我們一起走吧！我們可以循著軍隊要征戰衣索匹亞的路線，沿著納帕塔峽谷走。」

就在他說話的同時，父王走出蘆葦叢，說道：「拉達梅斯，我是衣索匹亞的國王。」

接著，蘆葦叢中又傳出一些聲響。顯然還有其他人也在偷聽我們的談話。

是安納瑞斯！她叫來神廟的祭司，命令他們逮捕拉達梅斯。她看起來非常地生氣。

她說道：「拉達梅斯，你背叛了我，背叛了自己的國家！我對你太失望了！」

拉達梅斯答道：「我會跟祭司走，接受懲罰。阿伊達，妳快逃跑吧！和阿摩納斯洛一起跳跑，現在就走，不然就來不及了！」

於是，父王帶著我逃進暗夜之中。

p. 112–113 當公主有什麼用啊？我痛苦得無法入睡呀！

今晚，拉達梅斯來到我的房間。我對他說：「愛我吧，我會去找我父王，求他大發慈悲，他會為了我饒你一命！」

但他卻只說：「安納瑞斯公主，妳有仁慈的心腸，但是我沒有活下去的理由。阿伊達走了，沒有她，我的生命就失去意義了。我聽說，她和她父親已經被抓到，被處死了。」

我立刻回答：「並沒有，她父親被抓到，但她逃跑了。只要你不要再愛他，我就會救你。我會好好愛你，就像她愛你一樣。」

他接下來所說的話，傷透了我的心。他說：「我永遠不可能愛妳的，安納瑞斯。我要走了，靜待死亡的到來！」

他走出我的房間，也走出了我的生命，自此以後，我就再也沒見過他了。他被關進神廟的地牢裡，他將會在那個冰冷孤涼的地方，悲慘地死去。

p. 114–115 我終於找到了一個能讓我感到快樂的地方。我回到尼羅河畔的神廟，因為我知道祭司會把拉達梅斯關在神廟地牢裡，所以我就先去地牢裡等他了。

我對他說：「拉達梅斯，吾愛！我來這裡和你同生同死！我們一起死吧，逃離這痛苦世界，一起到一個更美好的地方吧！」我們依靠在彼此懷中，終於能幸福相伴了。

祭司把拉達梅斯關進地牢已有很長時間，他現在想必已經歸西了。

我一直沒有阿伊達的消息。或許，他們兩個是死在我的妒恨之下的吧！我在不久後得知了她也是公主，我們本來是可以成為摯友的，但我對她不仁。

我夜夜為拉達梅斯落淚，如果阿伊達已經不在人間了，那我也會為他流淚。我願他們來生幸福！

157

Answers

P. 28 **(A)** **①** (a) **②** (b) **③** (d)

(B) **①** whisper **②** force **③** arrive
④ solve **⑤** fail **⑥** interrupt

P. 29 **(C)** **①** (b) **②** (b)

(D) **①** T **②** F **③** T **④** F **⑤** F

P. 44 **(A)** **①** Liu **②** Turandot **③** Calaf
④ Ping, Pong, Pang

(B) **①** I have promised to never allow any man to touch me.
② I am thinking of going to Greece for my next vacation.
③ I am looking forward to your birthday party next week.

P. 64 **(A)** **①** T **②** T **③** F **④** T **⑤** F

(B) **①** (b) **②** (a) **③** (c)

P. 65 **(C)** **①** barracks **②** begged **③** desert
④ coward **⑤** risk

P. 80 **(A)** **①** (b) **②** (a)

(B) **①** returned **②** will kill **③** replied
④ want **⑤** looked

P. 96 **(A)** **①** Amneris **②** Aida **③** Aida
④ Amneris **⑤** Amneris

(B) **①** I used to think that one day he would love me.
② It used to be easy to be kind and friendly to Aida.

P. 97   C ❶ F ❷ F ❸ T ❹ F ❺ T

        D ❶ miserable ❷ myself ❸ comfort
           ❹ army ❺ enemies ❻ honor

P. 116 A ❶ (d) ❷ (a) ❸ (b)

        B ❶ Amneris ❷ Radames ❸ Aida
           ❹ Amneris, Aida

P. 130 A ❶ She is a princess who loves a general. But he
              loves another woman. (d)
           ❷ People call her the ice princess because she is a
              cold-hearted woman. (a)
           ❸ She was a beautiful princess but now she works
              in the palace as a slave. (c)
           ❹ She loves freedom. She always decide who she
              loves. (b)

        B ❶ adventure   ❷ change my life
           ❸ wedding, funeral ❹ riddles ❺ devotion

P. 131 C ❶ Why didn't Don Jose run away after killing
              Carmen? (c)
           ❷ Why did Carmen want Don Jose to leave her? (a)

        D ❶ The princess Amneris was jealous of Aida
              because Aida was intelligent. (F)
           ❷ Amneris thought Radames would come to love
              her some time ago. (T)
           ❸ Aida was in love with Radames but she had to
              keep it a secret. (T)
           ❹ Amneris loved Radames, but she didn't want to
              break Aida's heart. (F)
           ❺ Radames wanted to marry Amneris because
              she was a princess. (F)

歌劇故事【二版】
The Opera Stories

改寫 _ Louise Benette, David Hwang
插圖 _ Ludmila Pipchenko
翻譯 / 編輯 _ 羅竹君
作者 / 故事簡介翻譯 _ 王采翎
校對 _ 王采翎
封面設計 _ 林書玉
排版 _ 葳豐／林書玉
播音員 _ Michael Yancey,
　　　　 Kathleen Adrian, Mary Jones
製程管理 _ 洪巧玲

發行人 _ 周均亮
出版者 _ 寂天文化事業股份有限公司
電話 _ +886-2-2365-9739
傳真 _ +886-2-2365-9835
網址 _ www.icosmos.com.tw
讀者服務 _ onlineservice@icosmos.com.tw
出版日期 _ 2019年10月 二版一刷（250201）
郵撥帳號 _ 1998620-0 寂天文化事業股份有限公司

Adaptors of "*The Opera Stories*"

Louise Benette

Macquarie University (MA, TESOL)
Sookmyung Women's University,
English Instructor

David Hwang

Michigan State University (MA,
TESOL)
Ewha Womans University, English
Chief Instructor,
CEO at EDITUS

國家圖書館出版品預行編目資料

歌劇故事【二版】 / Louise Benette, David Hwang
改寫. —二版. —[臺北市]：寂天文化, 2019.10 面；公
分. (Grade 4經典文學讀本)譯自：The opera stories :
Turandot, Carmen, and Aida

ISBN　978-986-318-848-3 (25K平裝附光碟片)

1. 英語　2. 讀本

805.18　　　　　　　　　　　　108016086